I0632852

A NOTE FROM THE AUTHOR

Thank you for reading **Saving You Saving Me**. **Saving You Saving Me** is a departure from the YA fantasy romance book series I usually write, but I felt I had to tell this story. Usually isn't that how stories get told?

Based on some actual events and from compilations of people I've known, **Saving You Saving Me** is a work of fiction, but contains realistic situations and issues, which will have themes I hope are presented as realistically as possible in YA fiction. However, because I'm a fantasy novelist, there may be touches of that as well.

Due to some of the mature themes contained in this novel, this novel is suggested for mature teens, young adults, new adults, age 17 and older.

I sincerely hope you will enjoy Sam's story. I am honored that you chose to read it.

Sincerely,

Kailin

Saving You Saving Me (You & Me Trilogy)

Saving You

Saving Me

kailin gow

Kailin Gow

Saving You Saving Me
Published by
Sparklesoup Inc.
Copyright © 2012 Kailin Gow

All Rights Reserved. No part of this book may be reproduced or transmitted in any form or by any means, graphic, electronic, or mechanical, including photocopying, recording, taping or by any information storage or retrieval system, without the permission in writing from the publisher except in case of brief quotations embodied in critical articles and reviews.

For information, please contact:
www.sparklesoup.com
Second Edition.
Printed in the United States of America.

Aspiring psychiatrist and high school Valedictorian Samantha (Sam) Sullivan falls for a deeply troubled young man named Daggers during a crisis call on her watch, which leads to the unraveling of her perfect world.

DEDICATION

To H.C.

Thank you for your bravery.

To all the volunteers who work at crisis centers, and the ones like me who worked as a volunteer or intern at battered women's shelters, mental health association, and the juvenile court; thank you for helping to make the world a better place.

Kailin Gow

Prologue

I'm standing here, holding a key; the one Daggers had given me before he left. "It's the key to my heart," he had said, pressing it into my hands. "You have my heart already, you might as well have everything else," he said softly as he kissed away my tears. He pulled me in close to his chest and held me tight. "We've come a long ways, baby. You and I. But we still have some distance to cover, hurdles to jump, if you want to." He laughed his soft gentle Daggers laugh that always sent flutters to my stomach. "I'm a many-layered SOB, a real messed up nut job, who others have given up on, yet you...you continue to peel away the layers." He played with my hair and kissed my forehead. I sighed. My multi-layered Daggers. Each layer more intriguing than the last, each one bringing me closer to the edge of no return.

"I want to peel away those layers," I protested. "I want to know who you are; deep down, if you'll let me."

Daggers closed his eyes for a moment and inhaled sharply. "I know, Sam, and I've been fighting it. If you knew what's really hidden behind all those layers, you'd stay away from me, as far away from me as possible." He opened his eyes to look at me earnestly. "You deserve to know, though. And I'm giving you that chance. With the key…the key to my safe deposit box. But once you know, there's no going back."

Chapter 1

<u>Two Months Earlier</u>

Monday

"Sammy! Sammy!" Nydia ran to me before she headed into her kindergarten class.

"What?" I asked, kneeling down so she could walk into my arms where I automatically pulled her in for a hug. I touched her braid and playfully used it to tickle her.

"Stop Sammy!" Nydia giggled.

"Not going to until you tell me what's up, baby," I giggled with her. Except for her green eyes, that mirrored mine…the exact same shade of deep green as our mother's, she looked like a smaller and cuter version of Dad with her dark hair and pale skin.

Saving You Saving Me (You & Me Trilogy)

Mom's green eyes peered at me from her sweet heart-shaped face. "Are you going to pick me up today or is Mom?"

I sighed. "I wish I could, pip squeak, but I have school stuff." I squished my face into as sad of a face as possible. "I'm sorry, baby, but Mom's going to have to pick you up like she always does."

"But I want you to," Nydia said. "Not Mom."

"Nydia," I said gently. "Mom loves picking you up." I tugged at her dark braids and whispered into her ears. "Besides, you promised to keep an eye on her," I said smiling. "For me."

Nydia smiled her secret smile. "Alright, Sammy. For you."

I touched the tip of her little nose with the tip of my finger, "I love you."

"I love you too," Nydia said.

"Now go in before you're late," I said standing up.

"Okay," Nydia hugged me again. "But I hate the way Mommy smells sometimes."

I cringed inwardly. "Me, too, pip squeak. Me, too." I pulled back from her hug and watched her walk into class. I was not going to let her see me upset. This morning was perfect. My life was perfect, and when I think about how sweet it is to be blessed with a perfect little girl as my baby sister, I thank my lucky stars for helping me see things will only get better. I pushed the negative sad thoughts out of my mind. I could not dwell on it. It did no one any good to dwell on it. I had to be stronger than that, to think of better things. Because no matter how bad it gets at home, I have my little sister who will always be there for me, and I for her.

As soon as she walked in, and I waved good-bye, I ran to my car, and drove as fast as I could to school. My meeting with our school counselor was early this morning, and I did not want to be late.

I pulled into the school parking lot, got out of the car, and ran awkwardly in my boots and skirt.

"Hey Sam," Gina from my English class called. "Happy belated birthday. The big 1-8. You're legal now! Whoo hoo!"

"Thanks," I laughed. "You'll be there soon."

"Sam," John Wrangler, a thin but tall guy from my debate class strode up to me and said, "Hear from the colleges, yet?"

I rolled my eyes. "It's still early. I have some time to get in what I need to boost my chances for acceptance. You?"

"Not yet, too. I'd thought you'd hear by now. All the schools would want you," he said nervously.

"Yeah right," I snorted. "My chances for getting in are just like everyone else's. Speaking of...I really have to get to my meeting with Dr. Green." I waved. "Good luck!"

I ran the rest of the way into the building to the offices, and into Dr. Green's office and sat down right when the clock on her wall struck 8:30 am.

Dr. Karen Green looked up from the paper in front of her. "Sam, let's get down to it. You've had a fine academic career at Cliffside Academy. A 4.2 grade point average will help you get in along with your high SAT scores, but you need something else to get a scholarship, too," Dr. Green said, tapping her long pink fingernails across the plain manila file folder labeled "Samantha Sullivan."

Inwardly I sighed. What else could I do to try to make it inevitable I could get a scholarship to Stanford? I'd worked so hard just to get the academic record I had. "Do you have any suggestions?" I asked my guidance counselor for three years. Dr. Green, with her messy brown shoulder-length hair, big hoop plastic yellow earrings, and black and white striped dress did not look like a counselor. The only thing that looked counselor-like on her was her smart chick glasses, the kind hot librarians wore. Who would've guessed funky Dr. Green was the best high school guidance counselor in all of Orange County, California.

"As a matter of fact, I do," she said getting up and walking over to a small black and white striped fabric-covered push-pin bulletin board hanging on top of a set of black metal-lock cabins. She reached over and unpinned a brochure from the board and handed it to me.

I scanned it quickly, before looking back up at her.

"Well?" she asked.

"It's a brochure for a teen call center," I said. "Sawyer House - a place where teens can call to talk about whatever problems they have without being judged." I looked quizzically at Dr. Green. Why did she hand me this brochure? Did she think I needed help without waiting to say it outright?

Saving You Saving Me (You & Me Trilogy)

"What do you think about volunteering there as a peer counselor, Sam?"

I swallowed. "I've never done anything like that before."

"Then it'll be a real experience for you," Dr. Green said, a glint in her brown eyes. "Look, Sam, I wouldn't suggest this to you if I didn't think you can handle it. You're an exemplary student, you've been class president of the junior class last year, you're active in your father's church, you're the school student ambassador…you're one of the most mature students in school."

Yeah, I also just turned eighteen years old so technically, I was a little older than my peers in high school. I blushed with Dr. Green's assessments of me. It wasn't something I strived to do. Being involved in school was something I'd done all my life, given I was a pastor's kid, and I had always been involved in one social activity or another. And the reason why everyone thought I was mature for my age…well, that was complicated, more complicated than I wanted to delve into.

"Um, Dr. Green," I said. "I don't know about this…I mean, I have a few things going on right now, and you've just said I'm already involved in some activities.

Surely that's enough to get me that extra edge to get into the college of my choice?"

"Stanford's very competitive to get in, Sam. All the applicants have grade point averages like yours. All of them have a few extracurricular activities. What you need to get into the same psychology program I went through as an undergrad, you need something like this." Dr. Green smiled. "Really, Sam, I thought you would've done something like this already. You're perfect for it." She took the brochure out of my hands and reached for her phone. "In fact, I'm going to recommend you to them right now. I know the director of the center, and she'll be delighted to have you." Dr. Green punched some numbers on her phone and waited a few seconds. Then she was talking. "Gail Reynolds, please," she said. "Tell her, it's Dr. Karen Green from Cliffside Academy." She looked over at me, smiling a "trust me, I know you'll love this" smile.

I sat back and watched her, trying to look interested. As she waited to be connected to the center's director, I glanced out the window of her office and into the hallway of the school administration office, trying to avoid her eyes, in case she saw the doubt in them.

It was a momentous glance, something I'm sure would have counted as one of the biggest moments of my life against which every other moment in my young life would pale. I did a double take as my eyes made contact with the coolest ice blue eyes I'd ever seen, and they belonged to Collins McGregor - the youngest mogul music producer featured on the cover of the latest issue of People Magazine. I felt my mouth dropped, but quickly recovered when Collins McGregor broke his gaze and a pink flush went up his cheeks.

He was better-looking than his photos, and I couldn't help staring at him, from his slightly messy wavy blonde hair, his sculpted cheeks and full sensual rocker lips, his tall and lean muscular body to his John Lobb-clad leather shoes. Dressed in a crisp white shirt and a silk small-patterned herringbone pale blue tie that matched his eyes, he looked every inch like a confident cocky young music mogul. Looking further down his tall and muscular frame was another story. Snug well-worn denim jeans hung off his hips in a sexy way that showed off powerful muscular legs and a tight butt. An expensive Italian black leather motorcycle jacket finished the ensemble. He was the picture of a hot bad boy music mogul. In person, he was gorgeous and stylish, exuding a confidence that permeated the room. Collins McGregor may be a music mogul, but he had the look and presence of a rock star. There was definitely something about him that kept me mesmerized. What was Collins McGregor doing at Cliffside Academy?

"Sam?" Dr. Green's voice interrupted my almost naughty thoughts of Collins.

I whipped my face so quickly from staring at Collins McGregor to Dr. Green's questioning face, I almost had whiplash. "Yes," I muttered, looking first at my hands and then at Dr. Green.

"Well," she said smiling. "You're in. You start this week. They had a peer volunteer who had to quit because she had to go back to college. They're understaffed and could really use your help."

"So when do I start?" I asked, shaking images of Collins McGregor out of my head.

"This Friday. They'll give you the orientation first and start you off with a practice call," Dr. Green said. "That's what Gail told me. You should get a packet in the mail in a few days with all the information." Dr. Green smiled a big Cheshire cat smile. "So, what do you think?"

I threw up my hands and shrugged. "I'll give it a try, Dr. Green. Thank you for getting me in so fast. I'm sure if you hadn't been involved, I wouldn't be starting this Friday."

"Oh, it's nothing," Dr. Green said. "I really think you have it in you to do this, Sam. You have to let me know how it goes…" She stood up, and walked to the door, signifying the end of our meeting. I stood up, smoothed out my navy pleated miniskirt, my soft pink ruffled blouse, and tucked my long wavy dark hair that came loose around my face, behind my ears, and walked out.

"Oh, wait," Dr. Green's voice called. I turned around, and she handed me the young adult center's brochure. I raised the brochure and nodded, turning around to head back outside. "Oh, Sam!" Dr. Green called. She walked towards me with my white cardigan. "You forgot this."

"Thank you," I said. Now I was going to be late for class if I didn't hurry out. I rushed out and bumped face first into something hard. When did a wall get put up outside the counselor's office? Then I lost my balance and landed on my butt, everything flying out of my hands as I tried to stop myself from falling harder.

Chapter 2

My hair fell forward, covering my face while my legs sprawled out in front of me, knees bent. My hands were flat on the ground, arms straight out, pushing my chest forward.

Gentle hands pulled at my arms, as a warm but firm voice asked, "Are you alright?"

I tried blowing my hair out of my eyes, but my long dark waves were too full and heavy to move. Strong fingers gently tucked my hair behind my ears and I looked up to see those icy blue eyes staring into my green ones. "Hmm?"

"You bumped into me and fell," Collins McGregor said, his face just inches from mine. Up close he was much more gorgeous than I could have imagined the president and founder of a music company should look like. His skin was flawless and tanned; his jaw strong. He smelled good -

an intoxicating mix of musk and vanilla. He was young, too – probably only 24 at the most, a few years older than me. His eyes bore into mine with concern. "Are you alright?" his sensual lips asked again. "Anything feel broken?" His fingers gently touched my elbows. "If you give me your hand, I'll give you a boost up," he said, straightening his long legs up from his bent knee position.

I reached up to give him my hand, but realized as his eyes briefly skimmed my body that my skirt had hitched up high enough to reveal my panties. Oh my God! My face burned red with embarrassment as my hand shot out to pull my skirt down. Of all the days, why did I have to be caught wearing my favorite ones, totally unsuitable for any guy to see me in – heart-covered boys-style underwear. "Crap," I muttered. "Tell me you didn't see that," I whispered blushing profusely.

Collins McGregor hid a smirk as he innocently said, "I have no idea what you're talking about." He reached up and grabbed my waist, pulling me up off the ground and into his strong arms. Again, I was facing him, except I had to tilt my head up higher to look into his face. He was at least a foot taller than me. He looked down at me, his eyes amused. "Well, Miss…"

"Sullivan," I said. "Samantha Sullivan."

"Miss Sullivan," Collins McGregor said. "Now that I see you're able to turn bright red with very little provocation, I must assume you're alright."

"That I am," I said smiling. I smoothed down my skirt, cursing it for not clinging enough so that it wouldn't ride up as it did. Great, so the first and probably only impression I had for Collins McGregor was that of me flashing him in my boy-style underwear. "Ah, thank you for helping me up, Mr. McGregor," I said.

It was Collins McGregor's turn to blush. "Oh," he said quietly, "you know who I am." His eyes went from interested friendly to frosty in an instant, guarded, as he said a little more stiffly, "I trust you don't make it a habit to bump into people."

I felt the ice in his voice like chips that cut through my skin. What happened to the friendly handsome young man who had just helped me up? "No, I don't," I said, matching his tone of voice. His face looked surprised, almost shocked when he registered what I said. "I only make it a habit to run into people's chests when they stand so rudely in front of a closed door so whoever comes running out can't help but barrel into them."

Collins McGregor's lips turned up into a smile, and he narrowed his eyes a little. "Touché, Miss Sullivan."

I flushed under his gaze.

"I don't believe I've said my name," Collins McGregor said, his eyes regarding me like a curious number on a spreadsheet.

"No, you haven't," I said softly, trying to stand my ground. Just because Collins McGregor was some hot shot boy wonder mega mogul, didn't mean he could intimidate me. "I..um…" Well maybe a little. "My father subscribes to some of the business magazines, and well…"

Collins bought a gentle finger to my lips then, instantly causing me to feel a heated tightening below my waist. I could feel my lips part slightly, and my breathing quicken. He was staring at my lips, his eyes had darkened, and I could feel his warm breath against my cheeks. Every nerve in my body was tingling, and I wanted to reach out to touch him, but I couldn't. I shouldn't. Not with him. Certainly not with him. Mr. Worldly McGregor was not just the cover boy for business magazines, but he was photographed enough at charity functions with a beautiful girl always by his side. "Can you keep a secret for now?" he asked, barely a whisper.

We were standing so close, staring into each other's eyes when a voice interrupted our mutual staring. I stepped back, putting some distance between Collins McGregor and myself. The air had become thick around us, and I felt tiny beads of sweat form around my chest. Was I actually burning up with heat from Collins McGregor? I gulped, disgusted with how my body was reacting to him. It was so instinctual.

I dropped my eyes from his to look at his full sexy lips, and I nearly lost my composure when the corner of it turned up into a small wicked smile. I was sure he was relishing in his effect on me.

"Ahh, Mr. McGregor, there you are. I see you've found Sam Sullivan, the girl who I suggested."

"What?" I asked turning around to see Principal Dean Lowry.

"Sam," Principal Lowry said. "Can you show Mr. McGregor around? You're the student ambassador and a senior so…"

"Miss Sullivan had already taken on the initiative to show me around, Principal Lowry," Collins McGregor said, standing next to me.

I gritted my teeth. Just because he's rich, handsome, and used to getting his way, Collins McGregor wasn't going to be able to get his way with me. He was the kind of guy my father warned me about. The thought of my father seeing me with a man like Collins McGregor sent chills down my spine. Involuntarily, I shivered. Collins looked at me funny for a second, and then his face cooled. "As a matter of fact, Principal Lowry and Mr. McGregor," I said. "I have a class I have to be at right now…I'm afraid I can't show Mr. McGregor around. I'm sorry."

Collins McGregor frowned, and Principal Lowry patted his shoulders. "That's fine, Sam. I'll personally show Mr. McGregor around. Now go to class. I wouldn't want you to ruin your perfect school record."

I gave an inward sigh. "Thank you, Principal Lowry." I turned towards Collins McGregor. His ice blue eyes bore intensely through me. What was that expression? Anger? Frustration? Even, maybe, desire? "Mr. McGregor…I hope you enjoy your tour."

Saving You Saving Me (You & Me Trilogy)

"Miss Sullivan," Collins McGregor said softly. "I hope to see you again."

"Oh, I hope so, too," Principal Lowry said. He turned to me and explained. "Collins McGregor is considering enrolling his brother here at Cliffside Academy."

I looked from Principal Lowry to Collins McGregor again. I almost said out loud, "Are you kidding? Why would a mega mogul want to enroll his brother into an obscure charter school like Cliffside Academy? There were more elite schools he could choose from." But I didn't.

As if he were psychic, Collins McGregor spoke up. "I grew up here, but didn't get a chance to attend high school. I thought I'd check out some of the best schools in town."

"Oh," I blushed. "You're here for your brother…"

"He'll be a freshman, 14 years old," Collins said, then pursed his lips.

"Miss Sullivan, Sam," Principal Lowry said. "If you don't go to class now you'll be late. I can give you a pass for this class, just for this. Mr. McGregor is a special visitor, and I thought you'd be the best person to show him around and to talk to him about our school."

I glanced at Collins McGregor, who stood with his arms crossed, looking at me with that look as though he was considering me for something. Then he smirked. At that moment, I wanted to wipe that smirk off his arrogant, but handsome face. No matter how much money he may have, I was not an object to be bought.

Principal Lowry must have seen my face frowning when he said, "that's alright, Sam, I see your reluctance."

I frowned. Was I that transparent? Principal Lowry was an on-again, off-again member of my father's church. I had to at least look like I was trying.

"But you have other things to do, I'm sure," I said, feeling like I'd disappointed Principal Lowry by not being able to escort Mr. McGregor around school.

"No, that's fine," Collins McGregor patted Principal Lowry's shoulder. He threw me a look of defiance before he put his arm around Principal Lowry's shoulder like they'd been friends for years. "I'd enjoyed your insight about Cliffside Academy (and the stock market), even further, Principal Lowry," Collins McGregor nearly winked at me. It was a sight that nearly had me giggling. Collins McGregor, young, tall and beautiful in his black leather jacket and tight hip-hugging jeans with his hand on short and bald Principal Lowry, who looked just as star-struck by the young and famous glamorous mogul as a groupie would with a rock star. Even Principal Lowry was intimidated. Collins McGregor said, "Lead the way, Principal Lowry."

Principal Lowry nodded, "Of course, but let me go get my coat first." He left quickly down the hall to his office, leaving me alone with Collins McGregor again.

"You're 18?" he asked.

"How did you know?" I asked.

"Principal Lowry mentioned you were one of the more mature students in school that I should talk to about Cliffside Academy to get a student's perspective. He also mentioned that he thought you would be interested in an internship at my offices in Newport Beach."

"He what?" I nearly snorted. Principal Lowry was trying to get me an internship with Mr. Collins McGregor?

"I knew you'd be surprised. He did mention your father is a friend of his, and that you're in need of a scholarship to go to college."

My face burned. First Dr. Green and now Principal Lowry. I mean I should be grateful, but I also didn't want the pity of someone like Collins McGregor. I was also embarrassed that my father would use his influence to get me an internship, even through Principal Lowry. "Sorry, Mr. McGregor, but I don't think…"

"Think about it, Miss Sullivan," Collins McGregor said. "It's just a thought, but the offer is there if you want it." His eyes burned into mine, and for a minute, I thought he was talking about something else other than an internship.

I shook my head. "I'm busy as it is, Mr. McGregor."

"It would pay for your tuition at college," he said.

I stopped. "You realize that's a lot to pay an intern?" I said, crossing my arms.

"You would be working on something complicated. Paying for your tuition would only be fair."

"I appreciate you offering me this, but I get the feeling it's for something else. I've seen pictures of you with pretty girls on your arm. I've seen how Principal Lowry seemed to eat up everything you say. I may know who you are, but I'm not impressed. You can't just walk around expecting to buy me, too. I'm not like that." I turned to walk away.

Saving You Saving Me (You & Me Trilogy)

Collins McGregor stood still for a while, his grin gone. "You have quite a low opinion of me, don't you?"

I shrugged. "I think you're arrogant and smug. You probably grew up with a silver spoon in your mouth and don't even know the value of a dollar."

Collins McGregor's face went from serious to hurt, and I immediately regretted what I had said. "I'm sorry," I said. "I shouldn't have…"

"You said what was on your mind, Miss Sullivan," Collins McGregor said, his voice tinged with sadness and anger. "But, you have no idea what you're talking about," his eyes flashed.

I swallowed. I knew I went too far, but he was such an arrogant good-looking golden boy with his millions, perhaps billions, heck gazillions, I don't know and I couldn't care less, that I had to let him have it. My mouth went dry, and I had to lick my lips again.

Collins McGregor's gaze went to my lips, and I felt a rush go through me as I saw him fixate on my mouth. I had heard of people having one-night stands, and although I could not understand it before, I now understood how people can end up having sex with each other only after meeting them within minutes. The way Collins McGregor was looking at me, and the way my entire body felt while he was looking at me, I knew why people could jump from "hi" to "bed" in an instant. I licked my lips again because of the nervous heat I was feeling. That was the kind of chemistry that flew between us. It confused the heck out of me, yet I could not ignore it. "I'm sure you have more to you than what meets the eye," I said, biting my tongue. I should stop before my curiosity got to me. "I wonder what kind of man actually has the need to constantly show off his wealth…come on, two beautiful women on each arm?"

Collins McGregor's face went white, and I could see the anger in his eyes.

"Sorry," I said again, biting my lips. I meant it this time. "You must have had your heart broken," I thought out loud. "Or are you overcompensating for some kind of deep dark secret you may have…" Gay? Small manly parts? The budding psychologist in me was piqued with curiosity. I had just read about Freud and his id vs. ego. My battling Freudian sides whom I named Lola and Susan were piqued. Something about Collins McGregor brought out the wild in me…Lola, while Susan the sane battle to keep my head on.

Saving You Saving Me (You & Me Trilogy)

Collins McGregor opened his mouth, and I expected a smart retort to come from him, but all he said was, "Hearts, that's my secret…hearts strategically placed can drive a man crazy." Then he fixed me with a look that could make a grown man wither and crawl away. "Miss Sullivan, for your information, and I think you should check your facts before accusing anyone of anything you have no idea about, I did not grow up with a silver spoon in my mouth. Quite the opposite, let's leave it at that."

I flushed with red hot shame as I looked at my shaking hands. Too embarrassed to face him, I walked away, my heart pounding with every step.

Chapter 3

I walked quickly out of the administrative offices and down the hall towards my locker, feeling my heart beat loudly in my ears. One more minute standing that close to Mr. Hot Bod and Brilliant Smiles would cause me to have total combustion. I hadn't let a boy affect me in this way since, well, ever. It wasn't the kind of thing I would do. It wasn't what Samantha Sullivan would do. The way I was feeling, if I got close to him at all, it would only lead to trouble…

And that reference he had to hearts. My face flushed for the gabillionth time today. I knew gabillionth was not a word, but the way my mind was going, I was going to have Tourette syndrome. Could I ever live down that moment when I flashed Collins McGregor my underwear?

It took me a while to make it to my locker.

"Sam!" Jennifer, my pretty blonde cheerleader

friend walked by with her boyfriend Rick Harvey, the star quarterback. Ever since she became cheerleader and started dating Rick, she and I grew apart and became preoccupied with other activities. "Just wanted to wish you happy belated Birthday, Sam," she said, linking her arm with Rick's. "I'm still bummed you did not try out for cheerleading this year."

"Busy with trying to get my grades up and other things," I said, noticing how Rick could not keep his hands off Jennifer. I gritted my teeth. College was the way out of my house, and I had to get a scholarship to go to Stanford, far enough away from home. But Jennifer did not know that. No one knew except for me.

"Seriously Sam, you are close to perfect in everything," Jennifer said.

"No, I'm not," I said, glancing at Jennifer who had slipped her hand into Rick's back jean pockets. I almost gagged at such public display of affection. "Uh, Jennifer and Rick, I'm kind of late for class…"

"Well…I'll see you around," Jennifer said.

I smiled and stopped walking then. "Thanks for wishing me a happy birthday," I said. I hugged her.

She hugged me back and whispered into my ears, "I

think I saw Collins McGregor come out of the principal's office with you. He is hotter in person than I expected. You are so lucky you got to talk to him."

I shrugged, glancing over at Rick standing a few feet away, who looked bored and was looking at his fingernails.

"You realized you were talking to one of the hottest most eligible bachelors in America?" Jennifer said excitedly.

I rolled my eyes. "Arrogant, too," I said.

"That comes from being a music mogul. Pretty amazing for someone who came from nothing, living off the streets, to being the success that he is. Arrogant or self-confident? Who knows, but he definitely has something special. I did not realize how young and good-looking he is."

"Me, too," I said.

"So what did you talk about?" she asked.

"Nothing," I said.

"I think he likes you," she said. "I saw him put his hand on your shoulder, and the way he won't take his eyes from you, it was intense."

Saving You Saving Me (You & Me Trilogy)

"Great," I said. "I'm not hoping to get married at 18," I said.

Jennifer rolled her eyes. "Who said you have to marry him? Seriously, Sam. You are too much of a PK. You're allowed to date, for goodness sakes, I hope. You have to have that before marriage. And marriage, that's totally jumping to conclusions. I'm not even thinking about that."

"Good," I eyed Rick picking his teeth. "I should hope not. Well, gotta go!"

"At least think about it if any chance it comes up, Sam. I worry about you, but now that Rick's my guy, all my time is spent with him or cheerleading. I hope you understand."

"Perfectly," I said, walking away to my locker. Now I was sure I was late.

I reached my locker in time for me to open the lock and pull out my books for the next class when I heard a familiar voice say "Hi, Miss Sullivan."

I jumped and my books tumbled out of my hands. Again. Collins McGregor was standing before me, looking every inch like a model for GQ. He had taken off his jacket and was now clad in his white shirt, pale blue silk tie and snug well-worn blue jeans.

"I didn't mean to scare you, Miss Sullivan," he said, bending down to pick up my books and handing them to me.

"I thought you were taking a tour around school with Principal Lowry."

"I did," Collins McGregor said, with undisguised annoyance. "We walked around campus, looked into some classes, and headed back." He added drily, "And talked mostly about stocks and the marketplace."

"Well...there really isn't that much to the Academy," I said truthfully.

"But you're here."

"I have no choice in the matter. My parents chose this Academy for me."

"Is it because it's academically challenging?"

"I think so," I said.

"Look Miss..."

"Call me Sam," I said looking directly in his icy blue eyes.

"Sam," he said, as if it were a strange word.

"Yes, Sam," I said, raising my eyebrows, cocking

my head slightly and opening my lips to inhale in defiance.

At that moment, Collins McGregor froze, his own eyebrows raised slightly. "You have very lovely eyebrows," he said, looking at my lips.

"Oh, thank you," I said, unconsciously raising them higher. I've never had anyone compliment my eyebrows before. With his eyes blazing on my lips, I felt even more self-conscious than before, which had the effect of making my mouth go dry. I stuck out my tongue and licked my lips.

Collins McGregor shifted his legs, and stood up straighter, his eyes darker than before. He cleared his throat.

"Sam," he said, "I need your opinion, as a student who goes to this school. Would you recommend it?"

"Of course," I said.

"How are the students here...any incidences of bullying?"

"We've had a few..."

Collins McGregor's face dropped slightly.

"It wasn't as bad as it sounds, though," I said. "The teachers, the principal, and several students stepped in. The bullies were asked to leave."

"Wow, that's intervention," Collins McGregor said.

"There's a school anti-bullying policy and stuff like that," I volunteered.

"Anything you don't like about this school?" Collins McGregor asked.

"The usual – better school food, more time to do homework, stuff like that," I said.

"What about friends?" he asked.

"What?" I asked, confused. "Do you mean is it easy here to make friends?"

"Do you have any?" he asked.

"Of course, I do," I said, offended he would think I was a friendless loser. "I might not have a lot, but I have some close friends. I'm not one to collect friends superficially. I prefer having a few good ones."

Collins McGregor's eyes went from mine down to my lips then. "What about guys?" he said.

"What?"

"Do you have friends who are guys?" his face was serious.

"I don't make friends with people base on their gender," I said. I was getting miffed now. I didn't know where all these questions were heading.

Saving You Saving Me (You & Me Trilogy)

"Good," he said. "It seemed like you're jumpy around them so I thought you probably didn't have a lot of experience being close to any. No brothers? No boyfriends?"

"I'm not 'jumpy' around guys," I said defensively. Just around you, Mr. Hot Bod and Super Inquisitive. "I do have friends who are guys, and yes, I mean, no – I don't have brothers."

"No boyfriend?" Collins McGregor asked. He was serious.

A sudden shiver went down my spine, and I involuntarily trembled. I didn't know what it was, but it was a feeling of fear and excitement at the same time. I shook my head. "Mr. Collins McGregor, this is getting too personal. And I'm afraid I've already missed most if not all of my next class. I have to get going."

"I apologize," he said, finally looking a little embarrassed. "I'll let you go, but…" he handed me his card. "I'm sorry if I came across sounding too personal, Miss Sullivan, but you seem to have drawn some conclusions about me already, as I've drawn of you. If you'd care to know, all you have to do is call or email me." He smiled shyly then, a smile that took me completely by surprise with how sweet and adorable he looked, younger even, like a little wavy blonde haired boy. Then he walked off.

I looked down at his card:

Collins McGregor, OWNER – The Collins Companies

Then in his handwriting in neat straight lines was his cell phone number.

This whole surreal meeting, this whole day was made real with Collins McGregor's card and phone number to prove it.

Chapter 4

I held onto the memory of beautiful Collins McGregor's face as I slid the key into our white Nantucket-style cottage house. It was the one thing I loved about moving to Newport Beach, California, five years ago when Dad got transferred to head up a medium size church in Newport Beach. According to him, it was something of a miracle, especially after what happened at his old church in the small town of Victorville, California - an incident that involved me and Billy Jackson when I had just turned 13 and Billy, was, well, 14, drunk, and a walking rage of hormones.

My face burned at the memory of the incident, Dad's face as he turned white hot with anger, and the deep shame I felt after he caught us. Ever since then, Dad had been distant from me, and I have vowed to work extra hard to repair my image as a Pastor's kid, especially as the somewhat famous Pastor Samuel Sullivan's oldest daughter.

The white wood door opened without a creak as I pushed my way into our comfortable, but immaculate house. "Mom!" I cried. "You home?" I didn't see her old white BMW in the driveway. She must have picked up Nydia and had taken her with her to the store. Getting a glass from the cabinet, I opened our refrigerator and pulled out the milk carton and poured. Only a little drip of milk poured out. They must have gone grocery shopping. With a growing five-year-old and a healthy teenager, our house always had milk in the refrigerator. It was the one thing my mother insisted on.

It was the one thing Mom was good at as a mom, making sure we had plenty of milk in the refrigerator. Other than that, I guess I got lucky with how I managed to grow up somewhat normal and get good grades, have dreams of going to college...

Then I noticed the dining room. Immaculate, as always, but I noticed the ring of a glass left on the table, a telltale sign, Mom had been drinking all morning long. And it wasn't just cocktails. She had been touching the hard stuff.

"Nydia!" I cried, running to her room and checking all the other rooms throughout. "Where are you?"

I ran outside to our tidied backyard where there was a swing set, a small flower garden, and a view of the canyons behind our house. Dad had spent a year fixing up the old cottage when we bought it just so we could have that view. A fixer-upper that had gone into foreclosure, we were fortunate to be able to snatch the little cottage for Dad's pastor salary in the expensive area of Newport and Costa Mesa. After Dad had finished fixing up the place with help from some of the men from church, the cottage was just as nice or nicer than the other homes on the same street.

"Mom?" I called around the corner of the backyard to the patio area with a gazebo. Maybe she had decided to spend the day reading a book out there while watching Nydia play. Please God, let that be the case instead of what I feared was probably true. I rounded the corner and she wasn't there in the gazebo.

My fear turned to dread as my phone started ringing. I knew it was Dad because of my caller ID. It had been years since I'd been close to Dad, ever since the incident with Billy. I don't know how I can ever live that down or move past it, but it's haunted my relationship with Dad, and I don't think he'll ever recover from it. "Hello," I answered. "Dad?"

"Sam," it was without warmth and had an authoritative and serious tone. "Where's your mother?"

"I don't know," I said. "I came home and she wasn't here."

"Has she been drinking again?" he asked, disgusted.

"I, um…"

"That sounds like a 'yes'," he said before he let out a loud sigh. "One of these days she's going to drink herself to death."

"I'm sorry," I said, sounding scared. I was worried for Mom, and I was instantly fearful of hearing Dad's strong disapproving voice.

"I tried calling her cell, but she's not picking up," he said.

"Shall we call the police?" I asked.

"No, she's not a missing person," Dad said. "Plus I don't want to answer to the police why Pastor Sullivan's wife was out drunk."

"Dad, I'm worried about her."

"Me, too, Sam, but she's a grown woman. She should know better." He paused before he asked in a voice laced with anger. "Is Nydia with her?"

"I couldn't find Nydia at home," I said.

"Holy…that woman! Doesn't even have the sense to know not to drink and drive. Now she's endangering your little sister's life, too."

"Dad, we have to find her. Where are you?" I calmly asked.

"I'm stuck in a conference in San Francisco that I'm speaking at. I can't get home until this evening." There was a pause. "I can't tell them I'm canceling just so I can go home to find my drunken wife. Maybe I can let Michael know, and he can help you track down your mother before she gets herself and Nydia killed."

"No, Dad, I can find Mom. No need to let Michael know. No one from church."

"Just in case, here's Michael's number. Do you have a pen?"

I grabbed one from the kitchen counter. Then I looked for a piece of paper that I could jot down the number on. The state I was in, I couldn't memorize the number if my life depended on it, although that was usually what I did – memorize phone numbers easily. I fumbled with my pockets and found the card Collins McGregor had given me.

I turned it on its back and wrote down the number for Michael, the junior pastor at Dad's church.

After I hung up the phone, I looked at Michael's number and thought about calling him. He was nice enough, with his brown overgrown hair and brown eyes. Even keeled, attractive in an academic nerdy way, and young for a Pastor at twenty-three, the teen girls and young women at church always giggled when he was around. Throughout the years, he and I had worked together on the youth program at church, and while we've been friends, I always sensed he liked me, despite his being older. It was something I wanted neither to pursue nor encourage.

I didn't know if I could let him know about Mom, though. Not that he seemed like the gossipy kind, but having been burned at our previous church after the Billy

Saving You Saving Me (You & Me Trilogy)

Incident, I couldn't trust anyone knowing about any of our family problems. Part of the reason why Mom drank so heavily was because of it.

No, I couldn't let anyone who knew Mom or Dad to know. I turned Collins McGregor's card over and was looking at his handwritten cell phone number. He had said to call him, if I cared to know why he was asking me about whether or not I had a boyfriend. What a way to get a girl to call you, right, Mr. Hot Bod and Getting Under My Skin.

So I called him.

Chapter 5

"Hello?" Collins McGregor asked.

"Mr. McGregor," I said, nervously. "It's me, Sam Sullivan."

"I know," Collins McGregor's voice said, smooth as velvet and a little shy. "I didn't think you would call me."

"Well, I'm curious about where you were going with all those questions back at school, but I have another reason to call, too."

"Hold on a second," he said. "I'm in a middle of a meeting. Can I call you back in a few minutes?"

"Sure," I said, a little unsure if I should be calling Collins McGregor about my problems. I mean, he was probably so busy, he didn't have the time to even eat.

Saving You Saving Me (You & Me Trilogy)

"Good, Sam," Collins McGregor said. "I've canceled all my appointments. I just need to get through this meeting, then we can talk."

"Here's my number..." I started to say, but he cut me off.

"I have it already, Sam. Five minutes to wrap up this meeting, and I'm all yours," he said with a hint of amusement.

Despite how anxious I felt about Mom and Nydia, I felt his voice caress me with the "I'm all yours," and I got an electrifying thrill that ran down my back.

What was I thinking? Collins McGregor probably thought I had called him for one thing and one thing only...

My cell phone rang, and the Caller ID was unlisted. I picked up. "Hi," I said.

"Hi," and I heard a smile at the other end. "Now Miss Sullivan...can you tell me why you called me?"

"I'm sorry you had to cancel your meetings," I said. "But I didn't know where to turn."

There was a change in tone, from amusement to concern. "Don't worry about the meetings. How are you doing? What can I help you with?"

"I figure if there's anyone who would know anything about security, it would be someone like you," I said.

"Yes?" He asked. "Where are you? Are you in any danger?"

"No, no, I'm fine. I just need your help in tracking someone who's gone missing."

There was a pause, and my heart began pounding. What if Collins McGregor didn't want to help? What if he thought I was some kind of imposition?

"Stay where you are," he said, "I'll come find you."

"No, I'm fine. My mother is the one. I can't find her, and she's not picking up."

"Sam, don't worry, my office isn't that far away. I'll be at your house shortly." Then he hung up.

He knew where I lived? If it wasn't for me knowing he was a mega mogul and probably had his security team check out anyone he gave his personal phone number to, I'd find the fact Mr. Hot Bod and Sexy knowing where I live pretty stalker-like. But wasn't that why I had called him?

Saving You Saving Me (You & Me Trilogy)

I went to my room, threw my school bag into my large worn but plush yellow armchair, and went to my closet. My room had the appearance of normalcy – white four poster queen size bed, white furniture, sliding mirror closet, comfortable yellow and white checked duvet. Cozy and comfortable, that was how my room looked like. I unbuttoned my skirt and let it fall to the ground. Padding my way to my closet, I pulled out a pair of folded stretched skinny jeans and shimmied my way in. Next I put on a pair of socks and black converse. I kept my blouse on and decided to pull my hair up into a ponytail. Next I washed my face, put on some lotion, lip gloss, and mascara. I wasn't dressing up for Collins McGregor. I wanted to look presentable and fresh, I told myself. Heck, who was I kidding? I brushed my teeth, too.

When I was done, I checked my phone for missed messages. No messages from Dad or Mom, but there was one from Collins McGregor.

Left a minute ago.

I listened to it while I put on a navy jacket.

"Hi Sam," the voicemail said. "I made it to your house and am standing in front of your door."

Oh crap! He was waiting outside. I ran and grabbed my purse from my chair and went to open the door after checking the window. Yup, Collins McGregor was standing in front, looking just as Adonis-like as before. Why was I so nervous?

I opened the door. "Sorry to make you wait, come on in."

He looked unsure at first, but decided to follow me in. "You've changed."

"I didn't want another incident with my skirt flying up, you know," I said blushing but smiling.

"No, you most certainly do not want that happening again," Collins McGregor said, the corners of his mouth lifting into amusement. He leaned his hip against the back of the sofa and looked at me, from head to toe with those amazingly intense icy blue eyes. "I like your hair up like that," he finally said.

"Uh, thanks," I said. "And I like you without your tie."

"You do, do you?" he said with that smirky smile. It was the kind of smile that looked like a prelude to a growl.

Whoa, I shook my head slightly. What is with Collins McGregor who could affect me this way? I decided to get down to business.

"Um, my mother, she's probably driving around right now with my little sister."

"And you're worried about that...why?" Collins McGregor asked.

"I'm not sure if she is driving around, but if she is...I'm worried about her state. She's not in the condition to be driving, which is why I didn't call the police to find her."

"So you called me," Collins McGregor said. "I see. You figured I would know how to find your mother, track her down."

"She's not picking up her phone," I said.

"Do you think she will have it on her?" Collins asked.

"I'm hoping she does."

"Good line of thinking, Sam," Collins said, cocking his head to one side.

"You can track her down, can you?" I asked a little anxiously.

"How do you think I found you here?"

"You mean you didn't know before what the address to my house was?"

"No," Collins said. "I tracked it from your phone. We'll do the same thing with your mother. All I need is your Mother's phone number..."

I gave him the number, and he was immediately on the phone, calling someone. "Howard, I need you to do a trace. The number's..."

I walked away, over to the kitchen where I pulled out a glass from the cupboard and turned around. Collins was standing there, his Blackberry in his hand. Surprised, I nearly dropped my glass, but Collins rushed over to me, bent down and caught the glass before he fell to the floor. I was stunned, as Collins McGregor stood back up and calmly placed the glass on the kitchen counter.

"Wow," I said, finally able to find my tongue. "You're very well-coordinated." Big understatement.

"I work out a lot, a habit I picked up growing up on the streets and having to be ready to fight," Collins said. "Besides it helps relieve stress, and I like the release."

Saving You Saving Me (You & Me Trilogy)

My heart fell, remembering how I'd accused him of growing up with a silver spoon in his mouth. I blushed. "You grew up on the streets?"

Collins McGregor laughed…a throaty deep laugh that sounded like a growl. "You look as though you're shocked," he said. "I had a rough beginning up to my adolescence. But that kind of hunger is what made me where I am today." He noticed my blush because he smiled, a sweet gentle smile. "Nice house you have here," he said. "Very family-friendly." He noticed Nydia's dollhouse in one corner, and the family photos lined up on top of the fireplace mantel.

"Um, I was about to ask you if you'd like something to drink."

"What do you have?" he asked.

I went to the fridge and opened it. I felt him walk up behind me, peering over my head and shoulders. My back stiffened as he stood barely an inch away. His presence was so strong, I felt there wasn't any distance between us. "Lots to choose from," I said. Luckily our refrigerator was well-stocked with tomato juice, lime juice, orange juice, cranberry juice, pineapple juice, sodas, and just about anything Mom can make cocktails out of.

He reached over my head to get a can of pineapple juice. "Your refrigerator looks like the mini-bar in a hotel room," Collins said matter-of-factly.

I blushed and turned around, about to tell him about Mom, but found my nose against his broad chest. He wasn't wearing a tie, and his shirt was unbuttoned down to the third hole, giving me a view of well-defined tanned skin and muscles. For a moment everything stopped, and I couldn't breathe. With my nose to his chest, I could tell his breathing slowed, too. I wanted to turn my head so I could rest my cheeks against his chest, to feel him breathe. His shirt was so soft, silky even, and he smelled so nice.

I hadn't realized I had my cheeks against his chest, until I felt his hand on the small of my back. His other arm snaked gently around my waist, pulling me into a hug. It felt so good to be in Collins McGregor's strong arms, held tightly like this. I did not know how long we were standing like this until I heard the phone ring.

"Hello," Collins McGregor said. "You've found her? Good, where is she? Okay, I'll head over there."

I looked up expectedly and asked, "Did they find Mom and Nydia?"

Saving You Saving Me (You & Me Trilogy)

"Yes," Collins McGregor said, taking my hand and leading me out of the kitchen. "We'll take my car and head out to get her."

And just like that, we were on Pacific Coast Highway heading in the direction of Dad's church. We got there, and there in the parking lot was Mom's car with her in it.

"Mom!" I cried, tapping on the film-covered driver's side window. I peered closer for a closer look. Mom was asleep. From outside, I could see Nydia sitting in the back in her booster seat. I tapped again, and Nydia began jumping up and down in her restrained seat. I could see Mom's head jerk up and then she turned it around to look at me sleepily. At the sight of me and Collins McGregor together, her eyes opened, and she opened the door, nearly tumbling out.

"Oh Sam," she cried. "What are you doing here?" Her green eyes darted between me and Collins McGregor.

"Mom," I leaned into her ears and whispered. "You've been drinking. You shouldn't have been driving."

"I just wanted to come here, visit your father's church. It isn't too far from home," Mom said almost slurring her words, looking very sad and miserable.

"But you had too much to drink. You shouldn't have driven and picked up Nydia this way." I instantly felt guilty, knowing Nydia had asked if I could have picked her up instead of Mom. But Mom should have known better. "Mom," I said gently. "If you ever drink far too much to drive, call me and I'll pick up Nydia. I'll drop what I'm doing and come get her. I don't want you driving like this." I patted Mom's arm. "You're endangering Nydia, too." I took a deep breath biting back the harsh words I would have let loose on Mom, had Collins McGregor not been a few feet away. "How long have you been here?"

"I don't remember," Mom said.

"Almost two hours," Nydia said from the back. "I'm hungry and I want to go home."

"Okay, then we'll go home," I said as I walked over to Collins McGregor who was standing by his sports car. "Hey, she's alright. She just fell asleep for a while that's why we couldn't get ahold of her."

Collins McGregor was heading over to Mom's car and reached it right when Mom got out to walk over to the passenger side. "Hi Mrs. Sullivan?" he asked holding the car door open for her.

Mom blinked as though she couldn't believe her eyes.

"Are you feeling alright?" he asked.

"I'm a little…"

"Mom's not well," I said quickly, hoping to sound convincing. "She shouldn't have been driving."

"Who is this nice young man?" Mom said. "He's very good-looking. Are you screwing him?"

What??? My mouth dropped wide open, not believing what just poured out of Mom's mouth. I looked over at Collins McGregor, and was mortified. He was grinning.

"Mom, this is Mr. McGregor."

Mom began imaginary fanning herself as she stared at Collins McGregor with a drunken blood-shot gaze. This was not how I wanted Collins McGregor to meet my mother, not by a long shot.

Next to me, Collins McGregor was still grinning. "Nice to meet you," he said, extending his hand to grab Mom's and kissing it. He turned to me, pulled me aside, and said, "Is everything alright?"

"Yes, of course," I said. "Mom's just not in the right condition to drive."

Kailin Gow

"I'll say," Collins McGregor said. "Can you drive her back?"

"Got that covered," I said smiling at him. I reached out my hand to touch his elbow. "Thank you for helping me, Mr. McGregor. I was…" I choked back tears, finally feeling the tension I held worrying about Mom and Nydia flow out along with the tears.

He pulled me to him and held me while I cried. "It's okay. It's okay, baby," he said, stroking my hair. "You must have been so worried." He continued stroking my hair until my crying subsided, and I got my composure back.

I slowly moved my head off his chest and saw that I had smeared his shirt with the tinted lip gloss I wore. "I'm sorry," I said, wiping his shirt.

"It's okay," he said holding my shoulders with both hands while looking at me. "Will you be fine enough to drive home or should I call Vincent, my driver to get my larger car?"

I took a deep breath and said, "I'll be fine." I smiled at him happily. What could have been tragic turned out well. Mom and Nydia were safe.

Saving You Saving Me (You & Me Trilogy)

Collins McGregor looked like he lost his breath as he kept staring at me, and I smiled back. Then he grinned. "Looks like you'll be driving, Miss Sullivan. Don't forget to buckle up." He shook his head before heading to his car. "You might want to prepare a glass of water, orange juice, and aspirin for your mother. I found that to be pretty effective for a hangover." He smirked, raised his attractive eyebrows and left.

Chapter 6

Friday

I hadn't seen Collins McGregor for over three days following the incident with Mom. He was right about Mom having a hangover and what to do about it. I wanted to call him to thank him, but I was afraid of what would happen if we saw each other again. After days of thinking about him, I had to admit I was attracted to him...a lot. And from the way he reacted to me whenever we touched, I would guess he felt the same way. For years since the Billy Incident, I hadn't felt this physically attracted to a guy. Well, actually, I'd never felt this attracted to a guy before, where every pore in my body just wanted to touch him. No one had ever had this effect on me, and I was worried. Worried that he was too experienced for me, worried about our six-year age difference. I was still in high school, although I was a senior and everyone thought I was mature for my age. He was a very successful music mogul at 24, who had already done a lot of things I had only yet to do. It was intimidating how much more experience he had in life compared to me, and I was afraid there would be too much of a difference between us.

I shook my head, it had only been one day...one long and intense day with Collins McGregor. I had let Lola, my primitive crazy inner pleasure-seeking diva or my id, as Sigmund Freud called it, have a field day lusting after Mr. Hot Bod. While it was fun and exhilarating, Serious Susan, my practical calm side or my ego, was telling me to get back to reality. Mr. Hot Bod/aka Collins McGregor had probably been caught up in the moment, as I was. Top executives of large companies tend to be very charismatic and driven in all aspects of their lives, according to Principal Lowry, whom I worked with in leadership training while I was Junior Class President last year. That was probably all it was... Collins McGregor was like a rock star and I was like everyone else when it came to falling under his spell. Heck, Mom, especially drunk Mom had, and she was like twice his age! The day I met Collins McGregor had been one long and intense day. He'd probably already forgotten about me.

As painful as that may seem, I had to find something that would take my mind off of Collins McGregor. I had to get back to reality and let Serious Susan back in the house or I wouldn't get anything done.

I looked down at my paperwork from Sawyer House, and I went through it all again, making sure everything was in order. Serious Susan had taken over and everything was neat and clean. I stuffed the paperwork back into the manila folder it had come in, checked my appearance in the mirror in the hallway from my room and headed for the door.

As I pulled into the parking lot outside a plain office building in Costa Mesa, I checked the time on my phone. 5 pm. Right on time.

I smoothed my cream-colored slacks and pulled my navy cardigan on over my white scoop-necked stretched t-shirt, an outfit I splurged on from The Limited. Despite being involved in school and Dad's church, I did not really have a work wardrobe. With the exception of a few skirts, blouses, blazers, and sweaters, my wardrobe consisted of mostly jeans, t-shirts, and sweats. Sawyer House, even though I was volunteering, was my first experience working outside of school and church. I wanted to make a good impression.

Walking up to the front door, I rang the doorbell and waited. A woman who was maybe fifty years old, dressed in grey slacks and a black blouse two shades darker than her fashionably styled chin-length hair, appeared and opened the door.

"Hi," she said smiling. "You must be Samantha Sullivan. Come on in."

When I walked through the door, the woman extended her hand and said, "I'm Gail Reynolds, the Director of Sawyer House. Dr. Green told me all about you," she said warmly.

"I hope all good," I joked.

"Definitely all good," she said, "or you wouldn't be here," she smiled drily. "Now, I bet you're eager to get started."

"Yes," I smiled nervously. "Before I forget, here's my paperwork." I handed her the manila envelope.

"Good good," she said, holding onto it. "Do you have any questions after going through it?"

"No," I said. "Not at the moment. I'm sure when I get into it, I will."

"Good, don't feel shy about asking. That's what we're here for. And call me Gail," Gail said. "Come. You can put your purse in my office while I give you the tour. We're pretty casual here. If you want to dress up you can or if you want to come in wearing shorts and a t-shirt, that's fine, too. We're not open to the public, and we don't answer to a corporation so there are no dress codes."

For the next few minutes, she led me from her office to the lunch/break room, and to the call center where there were volunteers in cubicles wearing headsets. "I take it, this is where all the action takes place," I said drily.

"Yes," Gail said, nodding at one of the volunteers who made eye contact with her. "Everyone you see here had been in your shoes. Now look at them, handling each call like a pro."

"I'd like to get to that point," I said, feeling Gail's enthusiasm rub off on me.

"Hey Gail," a friendly male voice said from behind me.

I turned around to see a tall lanky young man with curly brown hair approach us. He was wearing jeans and a plaid blue and white shirt and looked to be around 19 or 20.

Saving You Saving Me (You & Me Trilogy)

"Hi Derek," Gail said. "Come meet Samantha."

Derek reached us and he was tall, as tall as Collins McGregor, Serious Susan whispered into my head. Scruffy in a cute way, he looked like a college student. "Hey, Samantha," he said, extending a hand. "Nice to have you here." He looked over at Gail. "Is she replacing Joanne?"

Gail nodded and turned to me. "Joanne was the peer counselor who worked nights. She had to go back to school out on the East Coast. She's a psychology major at New York University."

"Gonna miss her," Derek said wistfully, but then he smiled at me. "But I'm glad you're here!" His boyish smile was contagious. I smiled back.

"Are you a peer counselor, too?" I asked.

Gail patted Derek on the shoulders and laughed. "Derek started as one two years ago, but he's climbed his way to training peer counselors now. He's one of the youngest ones we've had, but he's good."

"So are you in high school still?" I asked.

"Nah, graduated two years ago," Derek said. "I'm a sophomore at UC Irvine where I'm majoring in Psychology."

"This fits right in then," I said.

"Yeah, it's a good place for me to apply what I'm learning in college to real experience."

Gail touched my shoulder. "I have to get back to the Office and fill out some paperwork, but I'll leave you in Derek's capable hands. If you haven't figured it out yet, he'll be the one showing you the ropes around here. Just remember to drop by my office when you get ready to leave tonight."

"Thanks," I said, already feeling at ease at Sawyer House.

"Gail's really down-to-earth," Derek said when Gail was out of earshot. "You wouldn't believe she used to be a high-powered psych to the stars. Charged more than a top firm lawyer per hour for a consultation."

"Why is she here? Why did she give that up?" I asked, trying to picture Gail in a swanky office in Beverly Hills, sitting behind a desk while some famous celebrity actress sat on a leather chaise telling her all her problems.

"She wanted to help teens and young adults deal with problems they can't tell their parents or anyone else," Derek said.

"Did she start Sawyer House?" I asked.

Saving You Saving Me (You & Me Trilogy)

"She's one of the founders. It's a personal passion of hers."

"Personal? Why?" I couldn't help asking.

"The Center is named after her son Sawyer," Derek said. "Who killed himself."

"Oh," I said, suddenly feeling a deep sense of sadness for Gail. "I'm, ah, I'm really sorry to hear that." I was at a loss for words.

"Don't be," Derek said. "His death wasn't in vain. Gail's founded this Center in his memory ten years ago, and we've gotten tens of thousands of calls since. We'd like to think we've at least helped someone who needed it along the way."

Initially, I was hit with a sudden verge of tears, but the way Derek talked about how Gail turned around her tragedy into something courageous, I couldn't help but feel a sense of pride for being part of her mission.

"Do you want to grab something to drink before we start?" Derek asked. He took my hand very gently and led me to the break room. "Ta da!" he said, opening the refrigerator. Inside was a well-stocked beverage center with sodas, juice, energy drinks, and water. "Take a pick. It's available for everyone here."

Kailin Gow

I grabbed a can of Diet A & W. Derek grabbed a bottle of water. "Thought I'd show you that first before we head on into the conference room."

We made our way into a room with a large oval table and he gestured for me to take a seat. He stepped out and returned with a notepad, pen, and some papers. "You've read through the policies from the packet you received by mail, right? Here it is again…"

I looked at the copy of paper in front of me, reading through it, but zeroing in on three points:

1) Callers are to remain anonymous so they can feel comfortable talking to a peer counselor at Sawyer House
2) Everything at Sawyer House is to remain confidential
3) Peer Counselors have a choice to remain anonymous or not to the Callers, but we advise against getting too close to a Caller

Saving You Saving Me (You & Me Trilogy)

"That's there to protect the callers and to protect the counselors. Both ways," Derek said, noticing where I was looking. "Any questions on the rules and policies?"

I shook my head. I could imagine if I had any, I'll ask.

"Now here's the fun part. Let's go over the scripts. It's there so you have a guideline on how to answer questions." Derek looked at me for a moment and said, "I'm sure you'll do fine even without a script, you seem like the kind of girl who can handle yourself well in any situation."

I blushed, looking down. Was Derek flirting with me or just extra encouraging? Lola was intrigued, leaning forward in her black lace corset, mini-skirt, and thigh-high stiletto boots. Derek was boyishly cute and very nice. That's right – Serious Susan jumped in. He's more your type than Collins McGregor.

"Thank you," I said. "But I'd definitely feel more comfortable with a script around."

Derek grinned. "That's what they're there for."

I looked over the scripts and said, "Am I supposed to know all the different types of scenarios that would come up? There's cutting, divorce, bullying, bulimia, break ups, all kinds of stuff in here that I don't have the answers to, Derek. I mean I'm not a psychologist or a doctor. How am I supposed to answer their questions if I don't even know the basics of what they're talking about?"

"One step at a time, Sam," Derek said patiently. "We'll take it one step at a time. No need to feel overwhelmed right now. It's a lot to absorb. That's why I encourage you to go look up these issues on Wikipedia or Google it." Derek came closer and sat in the chair besides me, looking into my eyes. "You know, you don't have to start taking calls until you're ready. Even then I'll be around so you're not handling the call alone." He turned away and opened his bottled water, taking a sip from it. "I'm sensing you're not sure about all this?"

"No, no," I said quickly. "It's a lot to take in, and I wished I knew more about each of these topics so I could be more helpful to the callers."

"You can do that when you get home. Right now, let's go over some of the scripts so you have an idea where to start. He pulled a stack of multiple stapled papers, took the top one off the pile and handed it to me.

Saving You Saving Me (You & Me Trilogy)

"This one's about cutting," he said. He winced. "Self-injury. Do you know anything about it?"

"I know one girl who did it," I said. "She was much older than me at the time so I did not get to know the details, but I know it affects mostly girls than boys, and it usually affects teens. I mean I don't know adults who continue doing it."

Derek said, "You'd be surprised. There are adults who still cut themselves in order to relieve tension of extreme stress from abuse or violence. Usually the cutter uses a razor to cut themselves to cut through (sorry about the pun, Sam) their numbness to the traumatic event."

"Ouch," I said, wincing. "Why do girls want to harm their own bodies like that?"

"They think it will help them feel better. It's a temporary relief, if at all, and most cutters would agree it hurts more later. Some cut because peer pressure, others because it's the only way they can deal with something, when they can't talk to anyone about it." Derek took a sip from his drink and said, "So, that's why we're here. We're here for them to talk about whatever is causing them so much pain that they feel compelled to hurt themselves more in order to feel better about themselves."

"That's the opposite of what I'd think people would do when they're in pain," I said.

"True, but our mind works very strangely sometimes. It's a defense mechanism," Derek said. "But let's go through the scenario now you have more of an idea what cutting is."

He lifted up the phone and pretended to be on call. "Ring ring. Hello, you're calling Sawyer House. What do you want to talk about?"

I read the next line in the script. "Um, I'm not sure why I'm calling, but I need to talk to someone."

"Everything you say is kept confidential with us. You can talk freely with me. Why do you think you need to call here?"

"Because I'm cutting myself and I can't stop."

"When did you start cutting yourself?"

"Last week."

"What happened last week?"

"A group of my friends began cutting, and they made me do it."

Saving You Saving Me (You & Me Trilogy)

Derek stopped then and said, "there are many pages here on cutting, but I want you to read through it so you have an idea about what to say."

"And after that, you want me to read through this pile of scenarios, too, right?"

Derek grinned. "Right. It can take all night, but you get the idea. We are short staffed tonight so I have to be on call. How about joining me for this one call? You can observe me, listen in on the other headset." He stood up and walked to the door while I gathered all my papers together into a neat folder.

Derek led the way back to the call area, and took me over to one of the cubicles. He gestured for me to take a seat, while he rolled another chair over. "Comfy?" he asked, sitting down.

"Perfect," I answered back.

"Now put the headset on so you can hear the conversation." He put his headset on, and when we were ready, he gestured at a screen in front that was flashing green, indicating there was a call on hold.

On his phone, there was a button with the light blinking green. He tapped on it, and began speaking in a calm but friendly tone. "Hi, I'm Derek from Sawyer House. What do you want to talk about tonight?"

He was smooth, confident, gentle, and caring throughout the call. The girl, who calls herself Becca, said she was having a hard time dealing with some girls in school who started picking on her since she began dating their friend's ex-boyfriend. She felt ostracized because of it, and her friends who wanted to be as popular as these girls, ditched her to become their friends instead. She didn't know what to do.

"Are you still with the girl's ex-boyfriend?" Derek asked.

"No and yes," Becca said. "We just started dating but we're not officially together like boyfriend and girlfriend."

"Do you like him and want to be with him still despite the girls' tormenting you?" Derek asked.

"I do," Becca said.

"How does he feel?"

"I think the same," Becca said.

Saving You Saving Me (You & Me Trilogy)

Derek and Becca talked for 15 more minutes while he asked her questions, and she responded stiffly at first, but gradually became more comfortable.

"Then continue dating each other and forget those girls. If they start anything, walk away and don't get into an argument or fight with them. It fuels them. Go to someone of authority like a teacher, principal, or even your parents and let them know what's happening. Let your friends know what's happening so they can help stand up for you, too. And if you feel threatened in any way, go to your local authorities."

"Well, thanks, Derek," Becca said after a pause. "I feel better already, and I'll let my teachers and principal know before anything happens."

"Good luck, Becca. Keep calling here if you need to talk. You are always welcome. Remember, You have what it takes to change things."

"Thank you," Becca said shyly. "Bye."

"Bye," Derek said gently.

The green light on the button went clear, showing the Caller was no longer on the line. Derek turned to me, took off his headset, while I took off mine. "Well?" he asked. "What do you think?"

I smiled widely at him, feeling good about how Becca felt afterwards. "You're really good at this," I said.

"You'll be good at it too, in no time," Derek reassured me. "I've had two years more experience at this than you so I'm used to all different scenarios and issues. Not that everyone's problems are only statistics. They're not, but in time, you kind of figure out what to say."

I laughed. "No, you're just good at this."

"True," he admitted. "But what would you have said in that scenario?"

"Almost the same thing," I joked.

"Then you have good instincts," Derek said. "That'll get you through."

The green light came on again, and Derek put on his headset.

I placed my headset on, and listened in.

"Hello, you're calling Sawyer House. What do you want to talk about?" Derek asked.

A guy came on and said he liked this girl, but she did not know what to say to her, and if he should make the first move... Derek raised his eyebrows while I grinned.

Saving You Saving Me (You & Me Trilogy)

For the next 30 minutes Derek asked a lot of questions, but ended up answering more than half of them. I thought if I had gotten that call, would I be able to answer it since I was a girl, and just when I thought that, the phone conversation ended, and Derek turned to me. "In that case, if you get a call that you felt you're not equipped to handle, let me know or someone else. You could try to answer his questions or just listen to him," Derek said. "It depends on how much you know about...romance," he laughed. He stared at me. "What would you say if you had gotten that call? How would you advise a guy who finds himself liking a girl, even if he had just met her, and doesn't know how to proceed?"

Derek had stopped grinning and was seriously waiting to hear what I would say.

I smiled. "I don't have much experience in romance, really, Derek. I don't know how I would have answered."

"No," Derek said, genuinely surprised. "You haven't had much experience at all? No boyfriend, no dating?"

I shook my head smiling, feeling a flush cover my face. "I just never found time for it or was never that interested in anyone." As I said that, suddenly the image of Collins McGregor's face flashed in my mind. He was the first person whom I had ever felt a head over heels reaction to which I could not understand.

"Unbelievable," Derek said. "I hope you don't mind me saying this, but you're not exactly hideous or anything. You would have thought a girl like you would have your pick of guys."

I blushed. "Oh, come on, that's not true."

"Hey Derek, Sam?" Gail popped around the corner. "I'm heading out, but I wanted Sam to know how happy I am she's here." She gave me a hug, and handed me a vanilla envelope along with my purse. "Here are your copies of records, before I forget. And your purse." She looked at her watch. "It's time for you to head out, too." She looked over at Derek. "How did she do on her first day?"

"Brilliantly," Derek said, holding my gaze. "Just need to brush up on what each scenario is, and in no time, she'll be ready to handle any call."

"That's why she's here!" Gail said, leaving. "See you again in a few days, Sam."

Saving You Saving Me (You & Me Trilogy)

I nodded. Derek got up and walked me out of the building and to my car. "I think you're going to do great here, Sam," he said smiling. He opened my car door while I got in, our hands lightly brushing. It was warm, nice. "See you in a few," he said before he headed back into the building.

I let out a breath. Serious Susan was quietly applauding. I went through the entire night alright without thinking about Collins McGregor, except twice. Lola looked on, a pout on her lovely face.

Chapter 7

Sunday – Two Weeks Later

It was Sunday, and I was at Dad's church, playing the piano. I was not particularly good at it, but I knew all the songs because I have been playing the same ones since Dad was a pastor at a much smaller church. There he was in front of the church, a beautiful altar with a stained glass window depicting a scene with a Lion and a Lamb. Mom sat in the front pew with little Nydia, my beautiful little sister, dressed up in a sweet white puffy dress with a blue satin sash and embroidered blue flowers. It had been two weeks since Mom's drunk incidence, but I was still mad at her for driving herself and Nydia around fully intoxicated. What if something had happened? I wanted to let Mom have it that day when I drove her car back after Collins McGregor and I found her and Nydia at Dad's church. But she looked so miserable, and out of it, I held my tongue.

Saving You Saving Me (You & Me Trilogy)

I was glad Dad did not come back from the conference until late at night when Mom was asleep. He didn't say anything to me the night he came home, tired-looking and grim. He didn't say anything to Mom, either. It's been two weeks, and he still hasn't talked to Mom about it.

I watched Dad as the song the congregation was singing came to a close. Dad was a good-looking man with thick dark hair and some grey on his temples. The women in church thought he was handsome, and the men thought he was charismatic, confident, and successful, the pastor of a large church with a beautiful family. Mom sat in the front pew, dressed in a green sheath dress that matched her big green eyes, her full brunette hair long and straight, her pale milky skin almost wrinkle-free except for the ones around the edge of her mouth. Mom was a beauty in her younger days, looking like a 1940s pinup girl and always wearing bold red lipstick on full lips. She was originally from a small town in Texas when she moved to Hollywood to pursue her dream of being an actress when she met Dad. She could pass for being my older sister at times when she wore her hair down straight like mine or in a Veronica Lake wave. When I was dressed up with full war paint on including the bold red lipstick, everyone said I got my looks from Mom. Next to her was Nydia, looking sweet and charming in her dress. She had Mom's green eyes but Dad's coloring and a square jaw like Dad. She looked more like Dad than Mom, while I did not look at all like Dad. Getting up from the piano bench, and smoothing the skirt of my pink sundress, I walked over after the song ended and sat down next to Nydia.

The air between Mom and I was strained, but I made an effort. "Mom, you look nice in that dress."

"The Church Lady's Book Club lunch meeting is right after service," she whispered back.

"Ah," I said, thinking how ironic that Mom was The Church Lady, and how she kept a book blog called The Church Lady Blog, a blog that reviewed and recommended romances, cookbooks, Christian, children, young adult, and erotica books. "Which book is it this week?" I asked.

"A juicy one," Mom said. "Jane Eyre in Bondage."

I'd about bit down on my tongue and swallowed it, I was so surprised. Lola came out of her boudoir carrying a copy of Jane Eyre in Bondage, along with some accessories. Serious Susan had her hand to her mouth in shock. Me, too, Susan. Me, too.

"You got a group of women from church to read that for the book club?"

Mom's eyes glittered with glee. "Can't go wrong with a classic. And they loved it. Our lunch theme is Victorian Ecstasy – red velvet cupcakes, licorice shaped like whips..."

"Mom!" I said, loud enough for people around us to look our way. My face burned.

Lola was now sashaying around in six-inch heels carrying a red velvet cupcake in one hand and a ridiculously long black licorice in another, shaped like a whip. Serious Susan was in my worn yellow armchair, keeled over.

I was glad when service was over and I could head out, avoiding the eyes of Mom and the other ladies in her book club. Knowing Mom, she probably would have spiked the punch, too.

I took Nydia's hand to take her to her music class when I felt a tap on my shoulder from behind.

"Hi," a sexy deep, but young male voice said, sending shivers down my spine. Collins McGregor was standing there, looking like he came out of a magazine in his cream casual suit, white shirt, and Prada shoes. His wavy blonde hair was swept casually off his face, revealing his beautifully sculpted face, and his icy blue eyes that blazed into mine. I nearly dropped Nydia's hand. It was as though two weeks had not passed by since I last saw him, my heart was racing, and when he reached out to touch my hand, I felt the same electricity shoot between us.

"Um, hi," I said. "You're at church. Here. Why?"

"I wanted to see how it was. You know, when we came here on Monday to pick up your mother, I thought why not give your father's church a try." His eyes held mine, and the corner of his sensual lips lifted in amusement. He leaned in closer until he was whispering into my ears. "I wanted to see you, too." It was so low, so sensual, I couldn't take my eyes off his full lips.

I didn't realize my mouth had gone dry again, and I was licking my lips.

Collins McGregor's eyes blazed darker, and he leaned in to whisper. "Thirsty? I know I am…"

"Ah," Oh my. Hotness. All the blood from my brain left and my mouth was drier than before. Without thinking, my tongue shot out again to lick the perimeter of my mouth.

His eyes were so dark, so predatory, I felt that he would pounce at me at any instant. He took my free hand in his, and said, "Come on, let's get something to drink. I remembered passing a Seattle's Best on the way here."

I swallowed. It had been two weeks since I last laid eyes on him, and I had moved on - getting myself entrenched in work at Sawyer House, becoming good friends with Derek, even once going out to the movies at the Newport Beach Lido Theater with him. Derek was so surprised I had never been on a date, that he wanted to show me what I was "missing out" on. I agreed, but only as friends. I knew if Collins McGregor ever walked back into my life again, though, he would be the one I wanted to go on a real date with.

So here he was at my father's church, asking me on a date. "If you'll excuse me, I have to take my little sister to the music room. Want to come?"

Collins McGregor's face looked surprised at first and then embarrassed. "Oh, I didn't see you there behind your sister," he said bending down to speak to Nydia. "I'm Collins McGregor. How are you?"

"Hi," Nydia said with a mischievous grin. "You're very handsome, like a prince. Are you and Sam screwing?"

Gah! "Nydia," I said, turning beet red, "Where did you hear that? Never mind." I smiled and shrugged at Collins McGregor. "You just don't know where kids pick up things like that."

"Mom said it," Nydia said. "When you and Mr. Princely Lips picked us up."

Of course, where else would kids pick up sayings like "screwing" from? Their drunken erotica-reading moms. "Gotta love my mom," I said, hugging Nydia too tightly. I ruffled her curls and said, "Come on Princess, let's get you to the Music room. I hear they have a harp in there that you can play with."

"I want a drum set," Nydia said.

"We'll see," I said leading her to the Music room down the hall from the Sanctuary.

Collins McGregor's face was stuck in a state of amusement and something which I couldn't define. He followed me along the way, a few steps behind me, his presence as intense as always. Once I turned around to see if he was still there, and he just smiled, as we walked along.

Even behind me, I could feel his eyes blazing on me, and the thrill of that made Lola very happy, while Serious Susan looked on with caution.

After I got Nydia situated in the youth music class, I turned around to see Collins McGregor leaning up against the wall of the hallway outside of the Music room. He was studying my face, from my eyes to my lips and back to my eyes again. It was intense, and it was hot. It could be below zero and snowing in Southern California, and I'd be burning up.

"This is a nice cheerful music room," Collins said. "Did you learn to play piano at a place like this?"

"No," I shook my head. "Growing up, we didn't have a place like this. We had a hand-me-down old piano from Grandma that was always in the living room so I kind of taught myself how to play piano."

"Wow," Collins McGregor said. "You play rather well."

"Do you play?" I asked.

"If you can call it playing," he said shyly. "I pretty much taught myself how to play but eventually broke down and hired a teacher. I thought it would help me to wind down, but I find I'd like pursuing other means of release."

"Oh," I said softly, feeling as though he was implying something else. "You mentioned you have a younger brother," I asked. "Does he live with you?"

Collins McGregor's face twisted into a look of uncertainty. He didn't look like the Owner of Collins Companies at the moment, but the little boy with angelic blonde curls. How I wanted to run my fingers through his hair and pull him to me. Lola had her pom poms out, while Serious Susan had her arms crossed. My id and ego in full force.

"No," Collins McGregor said. "He doesn't live with me, but I'm trying to get him to. He's pretty troubled, and that's probably because he didn't know he had family." He shook his head. "Just a month ago, I didn't know he existed. I didn't know I even had a brother, a half-brother actually."

"You didn't know?" I asked. "That's pretty much a shocker."

"I'll say," Collins McGregor said. "But I shouldn't be so shocked. My father was a real bastard, knocking up my mother, and leaving her when he found out she was pregnant. It's no surprise he would have other unwanted children littered around. But my mother was no saint. She ran away from home as a teenager, joined a gang, and got pregnant with me." He smiled bitterly. "Not exactly the best way to raise a kid, and you know of course that I would have some issues," he said. He stepped back, his face disgusted. "I shouldn't be telling you this, Miss Sullivan."

I was about to say "No, it's okay" when out of nowhere, a big arm came around my shoulders and I was enveloped in a tight bear hug. Michael, the young pastor who was second in command at the church.

"Sammy!" he said, looking at me warmly. "I didn't get a chance to say 'hi' to you today. How's it going?"

"Well," I nodded. "Busy with school, trying to get a scholarship to Stanford, you know, the usual."

"Don't get too busy to hang out with me," Michael said, his face almost serious.

"Do we hang out?" I asked, smiling.

"Of course we hang out," Michael said, squeezing my shoulders, as he looked warmly at me, his chocolate brown eyes caressing my face with his gaze. He was cute, all right, and he knew it. All the women at church practically ate out of his hand. The young eligible bachelor pastor who had just returned from being a missionary in Southeast Asia. He was cute, but ruggedly handsome too, having blazed through jungles to reach villages where he would bring in food and medical supplies to people. He stepped back to take a look at me and laughed. "Sam, you've grown up before my eyes. I can't believe you're eighteen now, a woman, and beautiful."

"Why is it such a shock, Pastor?" I asked.

He shook his head smiling. "You've always been beautiful, but now, you're, uh, not a scrawny little kid."

I punched his shoulder. "I was when I first met you, Pastor, at 15."

"I remembered the day," Michael said, "And believe me, you weren't a scrawny kid back then, too."

I blushed. Of all the pretty girls at church and all the young available women, whose mamas were pushing them on the handsome young pastor, why did I get the feeling he kind of had a crush on me?

Collins McGregor had stepped up to Michael and me.

"Ah, Michael, this is Mr. McGregor. Collins McGregor."

Saving You Saving Me (You & Me Trilogy)

"Of the Collins Companies," Michael said. He reached out to shake Collins McGregor's hand. "It's a pleasure to meet the man who had been so generous in donations." He looked Collins McGregor up and down, in the way guys do when sizing up their competition. "I hope you enjoyed today's service."

"I did," Collins McGregor said. "Especially the piano playing part." He looked over at me.

"Sam is quite talented," Michael said, looking at me in admiration. He placed his arm around my shoulder and pulled me in close.

"So I've found," Collins McGregor said, his eyes looked at me possessively. His hands had bunched up into fists by his side, although he looked perfectly calm.

"Michael," I said, feeling Collins' eyes burning at me. "I have to go. Mr. McGregor and I were just about to head out."

Michael's eyes narrowed slightly then, and I'd never seen him look angry. "Sam," he said looking from Collins McGregor to me. "You're a grown woman now, just be careful. I worry about you."

"Michael," I said, rolling my eyes. "When have you started to worry about me?"

"I do," he said simply.

"Oh Michael, there you are!" a very pretty redhead in a white eyelet sundress walked up. Emily Johnson, a senior at UC Irvine and the head of her sorority there, glanced over at me. "Hi, Sam," she said coolly, before turning her attention to Michael. She stopped and turned around like a ballerina to look at Collins McGregor, and did a double take. "I know you," she said. "You're in the Newport News and all the society papers. You're Collins McGregor of The Collins Companies." She extended a hand. "I'm Emily Johnson." Her eyes perused Collins McGregor's body before reaching his face, and it was clear she had lost interest in Michael or whatever she was going to discuss with him.

Collins McGregor took her hand and shook it. Then he turned to me, grabbed my hand and said, "I believe we were just leaving." He nodded at Michael before pulling me out of the hallway, out of the church, and into his silver sports car.

He opened his car door and said, "Get in."

I slid into the passenger side, dropping my purse on the ground.

Saving You Saving Me (You & Me Trilogy)

He pulled the car out of the lot and expertly maneuvered it to head down the hill the church was on and onto the main street. He was silent for a while, his face expressionless.

"Um, nice car," I said. "You handle it well."

He smiled, the tension around the corners of his mouth gone. "Yeah, I like it. It's my baby. An Aston Martin."

"Like James Bond?" I asked, arching my eyebrows and cocking my head slightly.

He looked over at me then and there it was again, that look. Dark, hungry.

I licked my lips.

"Sam," he said softly. "Do you realize how sexy you look when you do that?"

"I didn't realize I was doing something sexy," I said looking at him with wide-eyed innocence.

Collins McGregor looked down and said, "Perhaps you don't. I forgot, you're so innocent. So young." He ran a hand through his hair, smoothing it off his face.

I couldn't keep my eyes off of him. His profile was as beautiful as a sculpted statue. His hair windswept, and that tortured look. Oh my goodness. I wanted to wipe that look of anguish off his face, to touch him, to kiss him.

"This is a mistake," he said, his eyes like steel as he resigned himself to a decision. "What am I doing? We should head back."

"Why?" I asked. "What is a mistake?" I reached out my hand to touch his on the steering wheel. My heart was beating so fast. "Tell me, Collins. I don't know what you're talking about. You're so cryptic, and I don't know what you want. All I know is that I haven't stopped thinking about you since we met." I used a finger to trace his hand on the steering wheel, and heard him take a sharp intake.

"Please don't do that," he said.

I pulled my hand away from his, and looked out the window. He sighed, but kept driving.

I felt like crying all of a sudden. I hadn't felt so much for a man before, hadn't wanted a man this much before to touch me, to kiss me. Collins McGregor with his Hot Bod and All Sexiness had swept me off my feet from day one and I couldn't help this longing, of wanting. "If you didn't feel the same, why did you come find me at church?"

Saving You Saving Me (You & Me Trilogy)

He kept his eyes on the road, but he glanced down briefly before saying, very softly, barely a whisper. "I couldn't stop thinking about you, too." He turned his icy blue eyes to me then, pinning me to my seat. He took a breath and asked, "Do you have any feelings for him?"

"Who?" I asked, too happy about him saying he was attracted to me, too.

"Michael," he said simply. "He definitely has feelings for you."

"I don't know why," I said. "I never once encouraged him…"

"You don't have to," Collins McGregor said. "Look at you. You're beautiful in a stunningly natural way. Your full shiny hair, your big green eyes, flawless skin, and perfect body…and you're sweet, smart as a whip, and sassy. You don't even know how special you are, do you?"

My heart jumped. He thought I was beautiful like that? I wanted to protest, thinking of all the flaws I had physically and psychologically. Don't forget mentally, too, Lola and Serious Susan added.

"So, answer me," Collins McGregor said. "I need to know if you have feelings for him or anyone else."

I swallowed. Such possessiveness. "I don't," I said. "I've never felt anything like this before, but all I know is that I want to get to know you better, I want to be with you."

Collins McGregor's eyes opened wide and shut closed before opening again. "You don't know what you're saying, so I'm going to show you, to put some sense into you so you know what you're getting into."

Uh oh. That didn't sound good.

"Where are we going?" I asked. "Are we still going to Seattle's Coffee?"

"No," Collins McGregor said. "I'm taking you to my house."

Chapter 8

I knew I should have said something, to protest about going to his house. It's what girls were expected to do. But having been thinking about him every day for two weeks, and burning with the desire to know him better, I went with him. But only after I called Mom and left a message on her phone. We weaved through Sunday traffic to head up the highway headed to Newport Coast where there were some of the most expensive homes in California. Finally, he drove up a winding road to a remote cliff, and a house, built like a modern castle. We drove through the black gates in front and turned the corner to the garage area.

He had a ten-car garage, bigger than my entire house. I gulped. His house reminded me of those homes you'd have to get in a helicopter up high to see all of it, courtyard, tennis court, mini golf course, basketball court, swimming pool, and all.

Kailin Gow

Collins parked his car in the garage, came to my side, and helped me out. "The previous owner seemed to like collecting cars," he said gesturing at the large garage filled with four cars - large black Cadillac Escalade, a red Ferrari, the silver Aston Martin, and an old beat up looking rusted red Toyota pickup, the words "ota" rubbed out so it just had the word "Toy" on it. "I only want a few," he grinned. "Cars are a weakness for me. Not exactly a vice, which I must admit to having quite a few."

"Really?" I asked, intrigued. Collins McGregor had vices. Who knew? Lola raised her hand, while Serious Susan said, 'That's why you're drawn to him, dear.'

Collins McGregor followed my gaze to the red pickup and said, "There's a long story to that which I'll tell you someday."

I thrilled at hearing him say "someday" as though it was a promise to be with me. Lola was grinning a sly wicked smile. I couldn't help smiling that sly wicked smile at Collins McGregor, dipping my face down and looking up at him with a look that asked him to come to me, to tell me.

Saving You Saving Me (You & Me Trilogy)

Collins McGregor stopped in his tracks and all my breath flew out my mouth, leaving my lips parted and my index finger in my mouth.

"If you don't stop playing with your mouth, I might have to join in," he growled low. Against his resolve, he rushed over, grabbed me around my waist and pushed me up against the fender of the truck, before he lowered his lips to mine, kissing first my top lip and then my bottom before using his tongue to open my mouth wider. He pulled my face closer as his tongue explored my mouth, making me lose all thoughts of consciousness. I moaned up against him, and he deepened the kiss while I pressed up closer, wanting more, needing more. My hands roamed his strong muscular back, from his broad shoulders to the narrow waist and hips. His tongue tasted so good, like honey as I touched it with mine, sucking hard on it until he was groaning and pushing his hips into me. He wrapped both his hands around my waist and lifted me until my legs were straddling his waist. With his mouth never leaving mine, he lifted me again, carrying me up unto the truck bed and depositing me on top of a soft mattress covered in flannel.

His mouth continued kissing me, but now his lips was kissing me on my jawline, neck, and throat, small fluttery kisses that made me want more. He kissed his way to the top of my chest before leaning back and unbuttoning his shirt, while keeping his blazing eyes on mine. "You're beautiful," he said before his tongue shot out to lick the skin around my neckline. "Flawless, like a porcelain doll," he said. "Just like I'd want my girl to be."

I shivered at his words. He felt me trembled and as soon as it all began, he pulled back, leaving me wanting more, but too afraid to.

He was breathing hard as he ran his hand through his hair. "I got ahead of myself," he said, "Come with me. As you know, Miss Sullivan, I'm in the public eye, whether I want to be or not. I'm also in a position where I have to be careful. My lawyers tell me I have to do this to protect my assets, myself, and my shareholders should any scandal come up. Believe me, this is the least romantic thing I've ever done, but having been burned by a former girl I dated once, I have to do this with everyone."

"Everyone?" I asked. "What do you do with everyone?"

"I have them sign a pledge. It's a sign of good faith. It's how I can fully let go of my guard."

Saving You Saving Me (You & Me Trilogy)

"I didn't know you had any," I said innocently.

Collins McGregor looked down before he lifted his frosted blue eyes to me. "I have quite a few. You develop that when you're on the streets, sleeping on the streets, and protecting yourself while you live off the streets. So as much as I would have liked to continue kissing you, I need you to agree on certain things in order for any relationship with me to work."

My head shot back. Lola and Serious Susan had their hands to their hips.

He lifted me up from the truck bed and led me into his house where there were travertine floors, limestone walls, everything tastefully decorated in an Italian Renaissance style. It was modern, classic, yet elegant at the same time. "You have good taste," I murmured.

"When it comes to women, hopefully," he said looking at me, his eyes still intense and burning. "I enjoy the classics, but all this you see here was done by Candice Berry, an interior decorator who's used to decorating the Ritz and other hotels."

"I love it," I said looking at all the golds, creams, and yellows that decorated the rooms.

"I haven't shown you the entire house yet so you

may reserve judgment until later," Collins McGregor said.

"All of what I see, I like," I said smiling at him, happy to be with him, having finally kissed him in what could be described as an incredible first kiss. My eyes darted to his sensual lips, and all I wanted to do was thoroughly kiss him.

Collins McGregor saw that hungry look I had on my face, and he tugged at me so that I was in his arms again. "So you want more," he growled, "happy to oblige." His lips were on mine so fast and so passionately that I was lost in his kisses, wanting more, needing more. He lifted me up again by the waist and carried me to a long low sofa covered in soft butter leather. He laid me down gently and proceeded to kiss my temple, my hair, and my lips again.

I was melting against him, I wanted to go beyond kissing. I unbuttoned his shirt, pulled it off, tossed it, and got rewarded with the glimpse of his bare tanned chest and rock hard abdomen. "Hmm, I somehow pictured you with less packs," I said, "but this is a pleasant surprise." I ran my fingers slowly down his chest, relishing the touch of his bare skin. "You must be working out a lot to get this," I said leaning into his chest to plant a kiss on his stomach.

Saving You Saving Me (You & Me Trilogy)

He inhaled sharply as I kissed him again and again. I could spend the whole day kissing him and feeling his well-sculpted chest and arms all the while getting closer and closer to the next step, except Serious Susan took over reminding me why I shouldn't let passion rule my senses. It was me who pulled away this time, harshly. Memories of me at thirteen, kissing a boy who was fourteen, French kissing, and touching. Everywhere. Then the shame. That look of hurt and disappointment on my father's face. The anger, too. Then the argument between my parents with loud shouts and screams. My mother in tears and my father furious. I shuddered, remembering how disgusted, how shameful I felt. Dad had taken me to the restroom to wash my mouth with soap. Since then on, I hadn't looked at any boys or tried to have any romantic feelings for them in case it became a Billy Incident. That was the day Serious Susan showed up, making sure to rein me from going too far or even to first base with any boy.

That was the day Lola, my passionate devil may care side, was banished to the back of my mind, never to appear...until Mr. Hot Bod with Smoky Eyes came walking into my life. "I can't," I said. "Not now."

Collins McGregor held my face in his hands as he

said, "Hey, that's ok." He ran his hand in his hair and stood up. "Maybe that's for the best. You're so innocent. That's what drew me to you, but you act mature for your age too."

"Are you saying you don't want to see me anymore?" I asked.

Collins McGregor took a deep breath before answering. "I don't want to, Sam. I don't want to stop seeing you. I keep thinking about you, though, but you're so pure, so innocent, I'm going to ruin you. I'm too dark and dangerous for you. You need someone like Michael."

"But I…" I felt so stupid thinking someone like Collins McGregor would like me, would even look at me when he had starlets and models hanging on his arms.

"Oh Sam," he said, sitting down next to me and folding me into his arms as tears began rolling down my cheeks. Serious Susan was horrified. I'd become emotional now. "Don't cry," Collins said, kissing away my tears and rocking me back and forth in his arms. "This is very hard for me, too, because I think we have something here, and I really want to have a relationship with you."

"I do, too," I murmured. "I'm not so innocent, I'm not a child, Collins." There I said his name without his surname. I was relating to him on his level, as an adult. "Please," I said softly. "I want to continue seeing you. We've just started, and I want to get to know you, find out what makes you tick, what you love, what you don't love…"

Collins chuckled. "Inquisitive, aren't you?"

"No, just passionate. I really do want to get to know you better. I like you a lot," I said.

"Then I'll show you what I expect from us being together, Sam. Take a look and if you agree to it, then we can continue this liaison."

I'd never been in a romantic relationship nor dealt with liaisons. I just nodded. "Ok, I'll take a look and decide." At this point, I was inclined to say "Yes," even if he purported to be an alien with two heads.

That was not the case, I thought, as he led me to his bedroom, which was covered in grey suede fabric on the walls, black carpeting, and steel chrome everywhere. On one side of the room, there were framed gold record awards. From his room, I could see out to the cliff and the Pacific Ocean beyond it. His room was on the highest floor of the house, and it had the most breathtaking view.

He opened the balcony glass door and pulled me out

to stand facing the ocean, a soft sea breeze flowing through carrying the fresh smell of saltiness and linens. "Would you like to sit here or come in while I show you what I want out of this relationship?"

Oh my goodness. I didn't know people had conditions set up before entering a relationship. This sounded like some kind of pre-nup, but before dating. This sounded crazy.

Collins came back with a cup of latte for me and one for him. "I was lucky," he said, "I caught Mrs. Anderson before she left to shop for groceries, and she made us some latte." He smiled his charming boyish smile that made him look closer to 20 than 24. I couldn't help grinning back, as I took a sip of the latte.

"It's good," I said. "Mrs. Anderson's a keeper!"

"She is," Collins said. "But I can't date her. She's married, but I can date you," he said smiling that sunny smile of his that had my heart melting.

"So, let's get this over with. What is it that you wanted me to agree to before we start dating?"

Collins pulled out a piece of paper and handed it to me. His smile was gone and in its place was a look of anxiety and nervousness.

I signed the first document after reading it through.

He seemed to relax after I signed the confidentiality agreement. I knew enough that it was necessary, especially for someone who was the richest and most eligible bachelor in the country, and if I wanted him to trust me, I'd gladly sign it.

The next document had me staring at the five conditions in utter bafflement. If I wanted to be Collins' girlfriend, it was expected that I:

1. Must keep my hair long and if I wanted to cut it short, I must get Collins' permission.
2. Must take care of myself so I look my best, and must get approval from Collins on the type of clothes I would wear when going out with him.
3. Must keep personal matters personal and not blab about it to the media.
4. Must agree to traveling with Collins and to attending entertainment functions.
5. Must be accessible to Collins by phone or person every night.

Kailin Gow

"I'm utterly baffled," I said throwing my hands up in the air, "how this isn't as earthshaking as I expected." I smiled at Collins, relieved it was not something utterly weird or kinky.

"Those are just my preferences, and it's an understanding I want you to have of my expectations. It's to avoid any conflicts later." Collins reached out for my hand. "Everything in life is a calculated risk...even relationships. In my stage and place, I can't even leave relationships to chance. I'm sorry, but my lawyers insist on the NDA." He ran his hand through his hair and said softly, "the pledge can be a written consent or an oral consent. I just need to hear it from you to know we're on the same page in this relationship. I mean, I hate to make this very formal, but I'm putting it out there as in any honest communication between lovers that this is what I expect."

You never know with celebrities and cell-phone tracing show-up-at-your-church mega moguls, Serious Susan pointed out, arms crossed, tapping her school marm oxford high heels on the ground. "Seems as though being in the spotlight, you would have to have an agreement for anyone constantly seen with you," I said. "I don't know,

Collins," I went on, "seems pretty normal to me, except the long hair part, first point."

Collins smiled a secret smile. "That's just so I can have something to touch and hold onto. I like girls to have long hair. It's a preference of mine. I find yours long and thick, very alluring."

"You're lucky I love my hair long, too," I said smirking.

Collins smiled a small smile, but still looked apprehensive and anxious. "Yes, I'm a very lucky man," his eyes twinkled with adoration, and he reached out his hand to touch mine. "I can't believe you don't have a boyfriend, at least one who would have shown you the world. You're too beautiful to be available."

I was blushing. Was Collins nuts? "You can have anyone you want," I said.

"No, not everyone," Collins said. There was that nervous anxious look again. "Sam, there's more on the back."

I turned the paper over and began reading. When done, my face had turned white. I looked at Collins again and saw the blood drain from his face as he noticed my pale face.

He looked so sad, so disappointed, as he led me back to the garage, to the Aston Martin. "I'm sorry," he said, "It's an addiction I've had since I was a kid. I know it's not what you're used to, but it's something I need, and I've come to expect in a romantic relationship."

I turned to him, my hands trembling. "I'm sorry, Collins. I can't do all of that for you. I know it isn't actually sex, but I just can't."

Collins looked like he just received the worst news possible. "Then I guess this is it," he squared his shoulders and became expressionless. He took out his phone and called someone named Vincent. "Vincent, I need you to drive Miss Sullivan back to her home. Not far. Pronto."

He turned towards me. "Vincent will drive you back to your home."

"Why can't you?" I asked, feeling weak suddenly.

Collins looked anguished now. "Because it's a clean break for us. If I get into that car with you looking like you do, I might as well kiss that pledge away. I need to keep my distance, Sam, for your sake and mine. And when you become who I am, it's no longer about protecting myself or you, but the tens of thousands of employees I have, my

- 111 -

companies' shareholders, and anyone associated with me."

"Is that what someone in your position does?"

"It's what I've learned to do in order to survive."

"Even when it comes to love?" I asked, tears spilling down my cheeks. I wiped away at them. This whole Collins McGregor thing had turned me into an emotional basket case.

Collins McGregor's face had turned ice cold frozen. "I wouldn't know, Miss Sullivan, I don't know what love is."

Chapter 9

Monday

It was a school day, but I was still lying in bed. I had been crying so much that my eyelids felt swollen, and my throat parched.

I still couldn't stop thinking about Collins McGregor, and my brush with Mr. Hot Bod and Sexy. Add Dark, too. I slowly got out of bed, willing myself to get ready. Serious Susan had taken over telling Lola to take a rest. Lola slumped into a plush red velvet chaise, exhausted from beating her chest and wailing.

I ran over what happened yesterday in my mind thinking how I would be able to have a relationship with Collins despite his strange needs. How could I possibly find myself able to fulfill them? It went against everything I was brought up to believe.

Saving You Saving Me (You & Me Trilogy)

A knock on the door, and then Mom's head peeked in. "Sam, you were extra quiet last night when you came home, is anything wrong?"

I caught a quick glimpse of my face before I answered Mom. My eyes were red and my skin splotchy, but other than that, I could pass as having caught a cold. "No, Mom, I'm alright, just not feeling well."

Mom rushed into my room and placed her hand on my head, surprising me. She hadn't done that since I was Nydia's age. Why now? "Sam, you feel fine, now can you tell me what's going on?"

"What makes you think there's something going on?" I asked.

Mom wagged a finger at me. "I knew you went out to Seattle's Best for coffee with Collins McGregor yesterday. Nydia told me, and even the look on Michael's face when he mentioned you and Collins McGregor said something else was up. Are you and that boy dating?"

"No, Mom," I said quickly. "We've just met actually."

"Then how come when you came home last night, you weren't hungry for dinner and you spent your entire night locked in your room? You didn't even bother coming out to hear what Nydia learned in music class yesterday. She was a little disappointed."

"Sorry Mom, not feeling well…It has been a long week, Mom, with me starting at the teen and young adult center…"

"All that call center stuff got you to stop answering your own cell phone, too?"

"Why? What do you mean?"

"That McGregor boy left five messages on our home voice mail this morning."

"What did it say?" I asked.

"To call him. All five of them," Mom said. "I erased all of them in case your father heard them."

I cringed. If Dad knew, he would not approve. I knew it with one hundred percent certainty. "Thanks, Mom," I said.

"I know your Dad and how overprotective he can be," Mom said. "You're his baby girl, and he took it really hard about the Billy Incident. We all did," Mom said. "But deep down, he still loves you and wants what's best for you. As do I?" Mom rearranged some of the pillows on my bed, and reached out to grab a brush to comb my hair in front of my bathroom mirror.

"Mom," I said, "I can handle this."

"I know, baby," she said. "You act so mature for your age, people forget you're still so young...like Collins McGregor." Mom finished brushing my hair and she began braiding it from the crown, expertly looping it into an elegant chignon on top. She pinned it with some rhinestone butterflies. "There, you look like a princess!" she declared.

"Mom, I'm not five years old like Nydia. I don't need to look like a princess. That's all just fairy tale," I said.

"Well look how pretty you look, Sammy Girl. We can see your long elegant neck now, and all of your face instead of having your face half-covered with your hair all the time."

"Thanks Mom," I said.

"I don't want you to grow up too soon," she said, picking out a royal blue ruffle tank from my closet that matched some of the rhinestones on the butterflies in my hair and jeans with rhinestones. "Now get dressed and tell me why Collins McGregor had left five messages for you this morning?"

I sighed. Mom wasn't going to let this go. "Mom, I'm not seeing him. We've just met, but there is something there."

"How old is he?" Mom asked.

"He's about six years older than me, Mom…about 24 years old."

"What does he do for a living?"

"Runs companies, Mom, some music ones. He's very successful at it," I said.

"So why did he make a donation to your father's church yesterday for one-hundred thousand dollars?"

I gulped. "One-hundred thousand dollars?" No wonder Michael recognized Collins McGregor.

"I don't know, Mom. Maybe because he can? He's pretty wealthy, and maybe that's how he'd like to spend it?"

Mom came over and gave me a quick hug…surprising me again with something she no longer did once I grew out of Nydia's stage. "I know Collins McGregor is charming, handsome, exciting, and everything that a girl wants, but he's also worldly and experienced. I don't know what you did or plan on doing with Collins

McGregor, but be careful, tread slowly, I don't want you getting hurt." She saw the tears forming in the corners of my eyes and pulled me in to kiss the top of my head.

"Mom," I said, "I haven't done anything with him, but I do feel something for him, and I don't understand why or how."

Mom laughed. "Well...he is very good-looking and exudes masculinity. He's the kind of boy who would make any woman weak at the knees. If you weren't affected, then I would be worried there was something wrong with you."

I laughed and shook her head. Mom and her budding cougar instincts.

"Now come on out and have breakfast. I made butter pecan pancakes complete with a whipped cream shaped face, scrambled eggs with tomatoes like you like it, and smoked apple sausages. The works, just for you." Her green eyes regarded mine and she said, "I'm sorry about what happened last Monday, Sammy Girl. Thank you for being the grown up."

"We had Collins to thank for that, too," I said, realizing how much I liked him.

"You're blushing," Mom said. "That McGregor boy has some effect on you alright." She leaned in and said, "I know you've been crying. You can't hide those things from a mother. Do yourself a favor and call him. See what he wants and deal with it."

"Ok, Mom," I kissed her forehead. "I will."

"Hey Mommy!" Nydia peeked in. "Wow, Sammy, I like your hair. You look like a princess. You're so pretty. Mommy, can you fix my hair like that? There's a little boy in preschool who has a Ninjago Lego set I want to play with but I think he needs to like me first for me to play."

"I'll fix your hair, but I'm not so sure about that boy, Nydia. Sounds like a player to me," Mom said walking out with Nydia.

I rolled my eyes and checked my iPhone for messages. Three missed calls. Unlisted number.

I searched for Collins McGregor's number on my call list and was about to press dial when I remembered why I left his place yesterday without agreeing to his terms of a pre-dating relationship. My ears burned thinking about it. Yay Collins had called me. It took away some of the pain, knowing he had not completely rejected me. But I needed some time to think about everything.

Saving You Saving Me (You & Me Trilogy)

Instead of returning his call, I came downstairs, had breakfast with Nydia and Mom. Dad was already at work, and I was glad since I was not ready to talk about Collins McGregor with him.

****

By the time school was done and I drove to Sawyer House, I was itching to call Collins McGregor to see what he wanted. While parked in the parking lot of Sawyer House, I checked my voice messages. He had left two more messages on my cell phone with the same message to call him.

Although I wanted to talk to him, I didn't want the immediacy of having to answer his questions, but I didn't want him to worry, too. I pulled out his card and sent him a text message.

TEXT
I'm not ignoring you. I just need time to think about everything. You have to admit, what you're proposing is unexpected.

Kailin Gow

He immediately answered me, which made my heart jumped.

TEXT

I'm sorry it came as a shock to you, but it's something I need in a relationship with a woman. If this is something you decide to do, I will explain in detail.

P.S. I miss you.

I smiled. There was something so lost about him that I could not leave him alone. Here he was, a powerful handsome mega music mogul tycoon who could have any woman he wanted, yet he was interested in me, an eighteen-year-old girl. The aspiring psychiatrist in me wanted to help him; Serious Susan wanted to keep him as a friend, while Lola wanted to make love to him in over a hundred ways. All three of them combined made me want Collins McGregor. Our heated steamy kiss in his garage and in his living room yesterday made me want to drop everything and rush over to his house to see him, but Serious Susan took charge and made me stick to my schedule – the second day at Sawyer House.

I got ready to switch my phone to vibrate mode instead of a ringtone and saw another text from Collins McGregor.

TEXT

Sam, I can't stop thinking about you, especially how hurt you looked when you left with Vincent last night. The last thing in the world I want to do is hurt you.

I saw how frightened you looked, and I wanted to assure you it isn't something to be frightened about. I'm not a monster, Sam. I hope you don't see me that way. If so, I'll have to do whatever it takes to change that. There is something about you that makes me care about what you think of me. I usually don't give a rat about what people think of me, but with you, it's different.

Kailin Gow

What I'm proposing isn't as bad as it seems. I'll have to prove it to you, show you it isn't. Whatever it takes.

Chapter 10

"How do you feel about being on a call all by yourself today? You've been training with me almost every day for two weeks. You are definitely ready," Derek said, after we went through script after script of scenarios in the Conference Room at Sawyer House.

I felt tired and exhausted, especially since I had been an emotional wretch just last night. "I'll try," I said with little enthusiasm.

"There is no better training than actual experience. Up to it?"

"Derek," I protested. "I need a break before we go into it. Right now I can't even keep my eyes from crossing."

Derek laughed. "Okay, break time. Let's get something to eat in the break room."

I put my head down on the table and closed my eyes.

"Never mind, I'll go to the break room," Derek said, leaving me in the conference room with my head down and eyes closed. I couldn't even muster up a mutter, I was out cold.

By the time I woke up, the room was dark and the blinds were closed. On the opposite side of me on the table was a can of Red Bull and a plate piled high with chocolate chip cookies. Oh my did the cookies look good. Taking a bite of the still warm soft cookies, I savored the taste of the chocolate chips melting in my mouth. I ate three more before I opened the can of Red Bull to wash it down. There was no ladylike behavior when it came to eating fresh homemade chocolate chip cookies.

The door to the conference room opened, and Derek stood in the doorway, his face in the shadows while his back was illuminated. "Oh good," he said, "you're awake." He switched on the lights and came over to sit next to me. "Why didn't you tell me you were too tired to be here tonight? I would have rescheduled you."

"No," I said shaking my head. "I need to be here tonight, Derek. I need to think about other people's problems tonight instead of my own."

"Oh," Derek said, with concern. "Do you want to talk about it? I wish you can trust me, Sam. I've been working with you and being friends with you for over two weeks now. I'd like to think we are good friends."

I smiled. "I can't right now. It's complicated. But we are good friends."

Derek laughed. "I'm good at untangling complicated. Look around you, Sam, this is what we do, and if we can't help our own, then what good are we with helping others?"

I regarded him curiously. I could not talk about Collins McGregor to Derek. Even if I could, I signed a confidentiality agreement with Collins McGregor. I opened my mouth to say something but shoved a cookie in instead.

"I'm glad you liked those cookies," Derek said, noticing four were missing from the plate.

"Oh, they're heavenly," I declared.

Derek grinned. "I'll be sure to bake some more next time you're here. It's my grandmother's secret recipe."

"No wonder why it's so good," I said, grabbing another.

"Sam," Derek said still smiling, "did you eat dinner before coming here tonight?"

My eyes widened. "Oh, I forgot. I was so preoccupied I didn't even stop to eat."

"No wonder you're tired and starving," Derek said. "Alright, tell you what. I'm due for a break so I'll run out and grab some burgers from In N' Out down the street. I would invite you, but someone has to be here until closing time, and there's only the two of us here tonight."

"I'll stay while you go on a burger run," I said.

"Technically, one of us is supposed to be on call, too, so we're ready to answer any calls that come in. Are you alright with that? Usually tonight around this time, there isn't much activity."

"I'm fine. I'll move over to your desk right now, so you know I'm good to go."

Derek grinned. "Glad your energy is back, Sam."

"Me, too," I said getting up and leading Derek to the call area and Derek's desk. Sitting down, I gave him a thumbs up after putting on his headset.

"Looks like a pro already," Derek said grinning. He touched my shoulders and said, "I'm heading out, but if you need anything, here's my cell phone number." He handed me a slip of paper with his number on it. "I'll be back soon."

I smiled. Being at Sawyer House tonight was the distraction I needed from Collins McGregor and his pledge as he called it. I checked my phone, and since his last text, I haven't received more messages from Mr. Hot Bod and Mysterious. Serious Susan was in her prime, while Lola was still nibbling on a chocolate chip cookie.

The screen above displayed a green light flashing that corresponded with the phone. I brought out my scripts and placed them neatly in front of me before pressing the green button to let the caller through.

"Hi," I said, "I'm ah Susan, what do you want to talk about today?"

A girl's voice said, "My name's Rachel. I'm having a tough time losing weight and it's making me depressed. I feel ugly and fat and undesirable. It's affecting my self-esteem. I haven't been on a date for months, and (I'm babbling too much, aren't I?) clothing looks too baggy on me. Where do I start? What should I do?"

I smiled. I got this one. It was one of my favorite topics to talk about when I was junior class president at school – Exercise and Healthier Food Choices.

"Nice to meet you Rachel," I said. "I'm happy you called because that's the first step towards weight loss and better self-esteem."

"What is your diet right now?" I asked.

"Mostly French fries and burgers, sodas…"

"Any fruits and vegetables?"

"I don't like vegetables."

"How about fruits?"

"Some…"

For an hour or two, we talked about the different fruits, vegetables, and exercise needed to lose weight, while staying in shape.

Finally I said, "Focus on losing weight by eating healthier foods – foods that have more nutrients per calories so you have more energy, rather than empty calories (I rolled my eyes upward thinking about how I just ate four cookies full of empty calories), eat smaller portions, and make sure you get physically active so you can burn calories off. There are many diet programs out there, but most of them have those underlying principles: eat right and exercise. Once you start to lose weight, you'll feel better about yourself. This causes you to make more friends, be more confident, and date more."

"Thank you, Susan," Rachel said. "That was really helpful. I'll start focusing on weight loss first."

"Total makeover when you do," I said. "It'll change your life. Good luck. Please call back when you need encouragement, too. That's what we're here for."

"Thanks, Susan. I will!" The line went off.

The green light on the screen flashed again, along with the one on the telephone. Having aced that last call, I picked up, feeling confident. "Hello, this is Susan at Sawyer House, what do you want to talk about?"

A muffled but deep voice inhaled a breath at the other end of the line before continuing. Since the calls were anonymous, callers also could call in using a voice scrambler device. It was something Gail believed in because she'd rather the caller get help rather than be concerned about the stigmas attached to whatever problem they're calling in for. "I'm calling because I have to talk to someone there, at Sawyer House. I mean, I feel uncomfortable talking on this line, but it's the only line listed."

"Were you in need of talking to someone in administration?" I asked, trying to sound professional. "They've left for the day. The only line open is this one."

"No, that's alright. I have to talk to someone or I'll go crazy. And your voice, it's so soothing, calming, and sweet. You've got a beautiful voice, one I can listen to for hours."

"Thank you," I smiled. "No one in admin is here right now, but you can talk to me. Maybe I can help."

"Susan, this is going to be hard for me to admit, but I think I have a problem with women."

"How so?" I asked, intrigued. Lola leaned in closer.

"Well, Susan, when I was a baby, I lived with my mother. She was seventeen when she had me. Gave birth right in the homeless shelter she stayed in after running away from home. When I was born, the first thing she called me was, 'Shit baby'. I was born to shit all over her plans in life. She called me other names, too, which I won't repeat. And she never held me, only enough to beat me. Other than feed me when she remembered, the only contact

I had with my mother was when she called me names or beat me. 'There you go again, dumb ass kid, shitting all over my life. I should have flushed you down the toilet when I could.'"

I closed my eyes, feeling horrified with what I was hearing. This poor man, this boy. I wanted to reach out to him, to hug him. No human should come into life to such hate, especially from their own mother. "Oh, I'm sorry," I let out.

"Don't be," the caller said. "I ran away from home when I was 13 years old. After being abused physically and verbally. I couldn't take it any longer. My mom, she thought it was amusing too when she would bring home women who would play with me, um, you know, have sex with me. I was popular with them because I was a pretty boy, and these sick women would pay my mother for me to do all kinds of things with them. Don't get me wrong, I learned a lot about pleasuring a woman, but I felt used and cheap. It's been several years, and I can't get over the shame. All my mom has shown me was hate, so I reciprocated hate back at her."

"Oh, I'm sorry," I said again, then clapped my hand over my mouth.

"I wasn't," he said. "I hated myself and wanted to kill myself a few times growing up because of it. She made me feel like a worthless piece of trash."

I had to ask. "How are you now?"

The caller laughed, a beautiful hearty laugh that sent shivers up my spine. Even with a voice scrambler, he had a voice that could have passed for Erik from the musical Phantom of the Opera. "I got over myself, if that's what you're wondering. It took years, and I'm still trying to find a way to accept who I am. I was pretty messed up."

I wanted to ask where he went to school, had he graduated, and where did he find the courage to overcome a childhood like that, but I couldn't.

"That's not why I'm calling, Susan. Here's the deal: my first girlfriend was the first person to make me feel like a human being."

"How?" I asked.

"She made love to me, made me feel valued, put up with me, and then she would talk dirty to me, call me things just to get me mad, and then we would make hot passionate love all over again. It drove me wild. The more she verbally abused me, the more I wanted her.

- 133 -

Saving You Saving Me (You & Me Trilogy)

"For some reason it turned me on. I know it isn't healthy, but that's how I am. She would call me to talk dirty, and from then on, I was addicted. It was a routine she had with me before we made love, and that's how I associate lovemaking with dirty talk." He paused, then said in wonder. "That's all that I know about being in a relationship with a woman."

I waited for him to continue, but he paused all of a sudden so I asked, "Have you tried forming loving relationships without having to hear your lover talk to you that way?"

There was a pause before the muffled deep voice answered, "I have, but it didn't work out."

I was not equipped to handle this call properly, but I kept on. "It'll take time to change something that you're used to, and I'm glad to hear you're trying. That's a start."

"But Susan, trying may not be enough…"

The despair in his voice made me want to reach out to him more.

"One step at a time," I said.

"One step at a time," the Caller echoed.

"Exactly," I said. Then I took the plunge. He needed someone to keep him accountable. From what he was saying, I was the only one who knew about his dark secret. "Have you tried going to a support group for this?" I recalled reading through my notes on sexual addiction a couple of nights before.

There was big sigh, and he said, "I can't. I can't let anyone know. I've worked too damn hard to get to where I am today to have it aired out publicly like that. I don't do group therapy."

I was right about my lost boy caller. I was his only bet to becoming whole, to kick his addiction. I was in way over my head, but deep down inside, I felt I needed to be there for him, to save him. Something about him made me feel as though I knew him, that it could be me in that situation, that we both had a sense of loss in us, the sense that we weren't good enough to be here, and we had to keep proving our worth. "Promise me you'll try, in your newest relationship."

"I promise, Susan," the voice said. "If I can get over this, maybe she would have me."

I took a deep breath and said softly, leaning forward, "I need you to succeed...ah..."

"Daggers," the voice said gently.

Saving You Saving Me (You & Me Trilogy)

"Daggers," I repeated, feeling the sharp sounds of the word cut into my tongue. I swallowed. "For my sake, as well as yours, I need you to succeed, I want you to. If you fail, Daggers, it means I fail…so succeed for me."

There was silence at the other end of the line for a short moment, and I thought he may have hung up. Then I heard a soft sob come from the other end of the phone line. "I'm sorry," he said in a strangled voice. "I just didn't expect that. No one's ever shown me that much care before. You don't even know me."

"I don't have to in order to know you're hurting," I said. "Something about you made me want to help you very much. I wished at this very moment that I could at least give you a hug."

"Ah, Susan," Daggers said. "You're an angel, you know. I don't care how you look or how old you are or if you are hunchbacked and hideous, you have the soul of an angel, and that's all I see when I hear your voice."

"Promise if you need support and encouragement, you'll call us here again."

"I will," Daggers said, "as long as it's from you, Susan."

"Anytime," I said. I felt as though I had been there for Daggers tonight. He seemed desperate to talk to someone, anyone. And I was in the mood to get lost in someone else's problems. Daggers' personal story had helped me forget about my own for a while.

Little did I realize, every day when I showed up at Sawyer House, Daggers would call, and we would talk for hours about everything – movies, politics, news, books, how he was doing with his addiction. Without revealing who I was, I would tell him about school, my sister's projects from school, what I was learning at Sawyer House, how I wanted to be a counselor, how I wanted to get a scholarship to Stanford, my dreams, my beliefs, how I wanted to someday soon move out of my parents' place and live with Nydia and raise her myself if my mother did not stop drinking.

I knew I kept Daggers occupied and distracted from thoughts of his deeply troubled past. But in so many ways, I was beginning to feel more relaxed about my own problems, having Daggers listen attentively while I talked. While trying to help Daggers over a period of a week, I realized he was the one helping me.

Chapter 11

Wednesday – 1 Week Later

Derek had brought in another plate of freshly made chocolate chip cookies tonight, which he placed in front of me as I sat down at one of the call desks when I walked through the door, arriving there right after school. It had become a habit of his to feed me chocolate chip cookies when I showed up, and eat them together with a glass of milk in the break room whenever we needed a pick me up after an especially tough call. "Some of these calls will get to you," Derek said. "We have to remember to be nice to ourselves and to support each other."

"You sound like a Renaissance man," I said.

"I am," Derek said. "I don't care about how I'm supposed to act because I'm a guy. I do what I do because it's the right thing to do as a human, not by gender."

Gail came by to greet me and to grab one cookie before heading back to her office. "You must be making a great impression on Derek here. He wouldn't let anyone touch the cookies except you, saying you needed it."

A slow flush went up Derek's neck and to his chiseled cheeks. "Gail's just jealous I didn't bake her a plate, but that's because she told me she's on a diet."

"And I'm not?" I asked, acting offended.

He looked me up and down in a way that made it obvious he appreciated what he saw. "Sam, you should be on a diet, a feed me diet. If you don't mind me saying it, you need some fattening up. I don't know if it's possible, but it looks as though you've lost some weight since starting here."

"Oh, I have a high metabolism," I waved away his concern, turning away from him to look at the empty screen in front of me. I had my own call desk now. A week ago, I was officially declared a full-fledged peer counselor, which meant I could handle all my calls by myself and that I could help other peer counselors with their questions.

Derek pursed his lips but didn't say anything. "Just remember Sam, like I said, if you need to talk, I'm here."

"Thanks for being here," I said standing and smiling up at him.

Saving You Saving Me (You & Me Trilogy)

He grinned back, smiling at me with warm eyes. "Anything for you," he teased. "I'm going to miss training you, but you caught on very quickly and went through training with a breeze." He smiled shyly. "I'm secretly proud of you. You've become a peer counselor faster than anyone here. And now you get to change shifts."

"Thanks to a good teacher," I said, using my hand to playfully shove him in the chest. He didn't stumble back, like I thought he would. Instead he grabbed hold of my hand and pulled me in towards him.

"I'm serious, Sam," he said, looking down at me with hooded eyes. "Soon, you'll be taking on another shift, and I won't be able to see you. You'll be on your own at your own schedule. You won't have the same one as mine."

"Derek," I said pulling away, but keeping my hand on his chest. "I'm sure we can have an overlap in hours."

Derek looked like he wanted to kiss me then. I didn't know if I wanted him to or not, but I pulled away. Spending hours with him had gotten us closer as friends, and I enjoyed hearing about his classes at UC Irvine and his desire to pursue a career in counseling. But I wasn't sure if

I wanted anything more than friendship from him even though he was very cute in a collegiate boy way.

He looked disappointed.

Right then, the green light began flashing on screen and on my phone. I turned back to the phone, put on the headset, and said, "Hi, you've reached Sawyer House, what do you want to talk about?"

I watched Derek sit down in a chair next to me, putting on his headset. He was going to listen in.

"Uh, I don't know where to begin," a young man's voice said.

"No hurry. Why did you call?"

"I did something bad, and I don't know what to do."

My eyes looked over at Derek, and his eyes met mine, calm and collected.

"Do you want to talk about what you did or about how you feel about it?"

"I want to talk about how I feel about it. I know what I did was bad, but I don't feel bad about it. What's done is done. I felt it was right."

"Then why are you calling?"

Saving You Saving Me (You & Me Trilogy)

"Because I know I hurt someone I cared about because I did what I did."

I took a deep breath. "Have you and this person you cared about talked about it?"

"Yes, and she won't stop crying. I feel bad for breaking her heart, but she's all wrong for me."

My face went white. Derek came over and took the headset off my head and placed the Caller's call on hold.

"Sam, are you alright?" he asked me.

I took a breath and said, "Yeah, I'm fine."

"Why did you turn deathly pale like that all of a sudden, Sam?" Derek asked.

"It's nothing," I said. "He, that Caller, just said something that reminded me of something, uh, someone I know."

Derek took my hand in his and said, "Was that someone you know?"

"No, not at all," I laughed.

"Do you want to finish the call or do you want me to?" Derek said, his face filled with concern for me. I couldn't help smiling back. He had become a pretty good friend in such a short period of time.

"I'll finish the call, Derek," I said calmly.

He looked at me intently for a second and then sat back down, while I put on my headset and pressed the button to continue.

"Hello?" the young man asked. "Are you still there?"

"Yes, I'm still here. I'm listening."

"So, should I continue seeing her, although I'm in love with her best friend and we slept together?"

The blood rushed back into my brain and my face was no longer pale white but flaming red. That was his problem? He cheated on his girlfriend with her best friend and now thinks it's okay to continue leading his girlfriend on? Anger surged through me for my fellow gender.

"Now listen here," I said almost calmly.

"Steve," he said.

"Steve. Listen. This is what you're going to do. You're going to come clean. To your girlfriend. If you don't, then you'll keep on hurting her, and it sounds as though you don't want that. Not to mention, you'll be hurting her best friend. If you love her best friend, you should be with her and not with your girlfriend."

"But Leila is pregnant," he said.

Saving You Saving Me (You & Me Trilogy)

I looked at Derek and rolled my eyes.

He sat back in his chair and actually broke out in a grin.

"Steve, is Leila your girlfriend?"

"Yes," he said.

Gah! I took my headset off, pressed hold on the telephone and began pacing back and forth. "Of all the…" I looked at Derek throwing my hands up in the air. "What do I say?" I asked.

Derek shook his head. "That's a pretty bad situation…one my frat brothers would all be shaking their heads at."

I glanced at Derek. "You're in a fraternity?"

Derek shrugged. "Yes, why wouldn't I be?"

"But you're always here, where would you find the time to be in one?"

"I should be asking the same about you and everything you do," Derek said.

"Derek," I frowned. "I don't have any experience with answering that one. What would you say?"

"If it was me, I would do the right thing," Derek said, "if I got the girl pregnant, then she shouldn't have to face raising a child alone, heck raising my child alone."

I smiled. Somehow his answer seemed so right to me at the moment.

I sat back down, put on my headset, and pressed the talk button on my phone.

"Hello?" Steve's voice asked. "Hello, is anyone there?"

"I'm here, Steve, and I honestly had to think about this before getting back to you." I took a breath before continuing. "Sometimes in life, we make mistakes...some mistakes bigger than others, while some are pretty small. Well...what you've done with Leila...sounds like you and she had enough of a relationship where you two once cared for each other. Now she's pregnant with your child."

"She didn't take her pill," he said.

"You didn't wear a condom, or did you?" I said, surprised I said the word condom. I gasped, putting my hand to my mouth. What would Dad say if he knew?

"No, I didn't think I had to," Steve said.

"Pills aren't 100% effective," I said, remembering what I read in a biology textbook.

"This is probably a conversation you should be having with your girlfriend and even both of your parents.

Saving You Saving Me (You & Me Trilogy)

Pregnancy isn't something to be taken lightly. There is another life besides both of yours to be considering too.

"There are adoption centers, people who would love to have a baby to love and raise, there are ways for you to help raise that baby together, even if you and your girlfriend aren't together. But you are still that baby's father," I said. "So act like a man and do what's right." I looked over at Derek who was watching me with a strange expression on his face.

"Gosh, well, I kind of knew that was coming," Steve said.

"If you did, then you already had an idea of what you had to do," I said.

"Yeah, it's just that I wanted to hear it from someone who's not involved at all. Everyone's got an opinion on this right now, and it's all so confusing."

"That's what we're here for, Steve."

"Thank you," he said.

"Best of luck, Steve. I wish you the best."

I pressed the button to end the call. As soon as I did, I fell back into my chair, letting out a breath of air.

Derek was quiet, but he had his eyes on mine as he took off his headset and came over to me. Before I knew it, he lifted me from my chair and pulled me in towards him, giving me a tight hug.

Bewildered, I asked. "What was that for?"

"That's for all the women in the world who had to face raising a child all on their own because some asshole like Steve couldn't face up to their responsibilities," Derek said.

Derek looked sad for a brief moment so I returned his hug.

"You handled that like a pro, Sam. You're really good at this, so good I forget you're only eighteen."

"I know, Derek, everyone's said I'm mature for my age."

"Oh, I don't know about that, Sam, just a few days ago you were wearing butterflies in your hair like a little girl."

"My mother made up my hair that day. They're my baby sister's hairclips," I blushed, embarrassed to be caught wearing my baby sister's hair accessories. "So maybe I don't have a sophisticated fashion sense…"

Saving You Saving Me (You & Me Trilogy)

"You looked adorable, Sam, as you should," he squeezed my shoulders.

"Derek, you are too nice. I bet if I wore a burlap bag as a dress and had knots in my hair, you'd think I look adorable."

He had a puppy dog look on his face when he said, "Maybe. The burlap dress I can see, but not the knots in your hair."

"Yeah right." He was such a nice guy. "Derek?" I asked. "This last call...you had a look on your face...like you were sad. Can I ask why?"

Derek looked so surprised that his mouth fell open. "You caught me off guard, Sam. You seemed so innocent, yet you're wise at the same time. I thought whatever was bothering you had something to do with that call, but the opposite was true. It hit home for me, what Steve and Leila was going through."

"How? Someone in your fraternity got a girl pregnant?"

"I wouldn't be surprised if they did," Derek laughed. "But no, it's not that. The reason why I was sad for a moment was because I was raised by a single mother. It was hard for her, but she was able to raise me, while going to school and working full time. She recently finished getting her Master's Degree in Education – I'm so proud of her. It was her dream come true."

I squeezed his hand and said, "You have an amazing mother, Derek. No wonder you turned out awesome!"

"Awesome?" Derek asked

"Awesomesauce," I said, shrugging. "Gosh, you got to get out more."

Derek raised his eyebrows. "But I do, Sam. I do. I'm in a fraternity in college, what do you think I do?"

My eyes opened wide for a moment before my hand shot out to clap my mouth. "I didn't think you…"

"I don't have a girlfriend like Steve does," Derek said, "but I'm pretty careful."

My mouth gaped as I shook my head. "Derek, you're a serial dater. Who would have thought?"

Derek looked hurt. "I am not. I just haven't found a girl who I want to date long-term."

"Fair enough," I muttered. "You're still a serial dater. Ha ha."

Saving You Saving Me (You & Me Trilogy)

"Just wait until you go to college, there are so many people there, you wouldn't want to settle."

I rolled my eyes at him, and he rolled his eyes back. We were being immature, rolling our eyes at each other until he stood up straight and reached into his pocket for his cell phone. "Hi," he said, his voice softening. "Kristen, I'm sorry, I forgot. The function is when?"

Derek looked at me and raised his hand in the air as if he was apologizing for taking this call. He walked away into the Conference Room.

I sat back down at my desk, and noticed a green light flashing on screen. I put my headset on and pressed the button.

"Hi, you've reached Sawyer House, what do you want to talk about?"

"Hi, Susan," a deep muffled voice asked. "This is Daggers. I've been waiting to call you."

I stopped. Almost breathless. Daggers. "I've been waiting for you to call," I laughed.

There was a gasp at the other end of the phone. "You should bottle that laugh and sell it. It's happiness in a bottle, Susan."

"You're kidding me, aren't you?" I said laughing again. "It feels good to hear your voice," I said.

"There you go again with that laugh," Daggers said softly. "They should call Sawyer House, Laughter House, it's where you go to get a quick dose of sunshine, at least for me, it is, Susan." His voice was so sincere and joyful.

"I hope so," I said, flattered and touched.

"Susan, I love hearing your voice. You know, I haven't call for a while, but all those times I called and we talked has meant a lot to me."

"Daggers," I caught my breath. I honestly could not breathe at that moment. "It meant a lot to me, too."

"How are things with you at home?" Daggers asked. "Is your mother staying sober?"

"She's trying," I said.

"What about your father? Is he talking to your mother again?"

"They talk, but I can see how Dad has not forgiven Mom for driving drunk."

"I'm sorry to hear all that, Susan," Daggers said.

Saving You Saving Me (You & Me Trilogy)

"That's how it is," I said before jumping into his problem. "How's everything going, Daggers?" I put on my Serious Susan expression.

"Ah the usual - me fighting against the dark. And floundering badly. I'm like a blind man clutching in the dark for a light that would never be. Whenever I think about going into a relationship, it scares the shit out of me. With the amount of baggage I have, I don't think any woman in her right mind would look at me twice. I realize I keep looking for women who would put me down and make me feel as bad as my mother."

My heart twisted again, thinking about the poor defenseless baby who had to endure nothing but hate from his own mother every day of his first two years of life. What person wouldn't be a walking case of poor self-esteem.

"Are you seeing anyone right now?" I asked. "How is it working out with the girl you're crazy about?"

Daggers said. "We began dating a few weeks back. She was so special, and not at all like the women I've seen in the past. She's pure goodness and innocence. I wanted her normalcy, I wanted to make things work with her, but I

Kailin Gow

think I blew it. She wasn't into what I wanted." He said so softly, "I'd give anything to have a normal relationship."

More than normal dear, I thought. You needed someone with a lot of love to give. Of anyone I'd ever known, Daggers was the one person who would need a lifetime of love to get over something like his childhood.

"Susan?" Daggers asked, he had taken off the voice scrambler device, and was speaking in his own voice, which was sweet, deep, and so sexy. I jumped. I didn't think I would respond that way to just his voice.

"Yes, Daggers?"

"I can't see you, but since we last talked on the phone, and I heard your voice, I thought this woman had the voice of an angel. I was taken aback after the call, I sat there for hours going over what we'd talked about and how you said everything. I don't think you have a bone in your body that's capable of saying degrading, abusive things like the women I've had relationships with."

"It's possible to find women who don't abuse men," I said. "Most women don't."

Saving You Saving Me (You & Me Trilogy)

"That's just my problem, Susan," Daggers said in his low sexy voice. Oh my goodness, Lola was licking her lips.

"What problem is that?"

He paused and then there was this excruciating groan. "I hate it, but I crave it, too. And I can't seem to stop."

"You've got to stop, Daggers," I said, trying to sound firm. "If you don't, one of these days, you'll get hurt or killed."

"I don't know if I can, Susan," Daggers said in a voice so soft, so small, like a lost little boy's. "What my mother did to me as a boy, with those women…" He began crying.

I began crying along with him. "It's okay, Daggers. I'm here," I said gently. "You will get through this…with me."

Chapter 12

Thursday

The next night, Daggers called again. "Hi Susan," he said. "I began dreaming of a better life."

"That's wonderful. What was it about?"

"I stopped being in an abusive relationship. I found a girl who I could love and who would love me back with all my flaws and deep dark secrets."

"I'm happy you're having these dreams," I said.

"The girl in the dream, Susan, has your voice," Daggers added.

"Is she pretty and nice, too?" I asked.

"She's gorgeous, the most beautiful girl I've ever seen," Daggers said.

"As long as she makes you happy and treats you like the beautiful human being that you are, I'm fine with it," I said, thinking I would be. But deep down inside, I felt a pang of jealousy that Daggers would be off falling in love with some girl who did not even know him like I did. I felt proud of his progress, but sad at the same time, thinking that as Daggers got better, he would no longer reach out for me.

Friday

Daggers called me on Friday with some news. "Susan, I'm happy to say my shrink says I've made improvements with my abusive relationship issue."

"You have a shrink?" I asked.

"Had one for a few years," he said.

"Then why did you start calling Sawyer House?" I asked. "Not that you're not welcome, but because we're usually the first person callers would call."

"I was looking for someone who worked there, and ended up talking to you." Daggers chuckled. "Good thing, too. You've helped me make significant improvements."

"Well, are you going to stop calling Sawyer House now?" I asked, feeling like my heart would break if he did.

"I should so you can use the time you talk to me on someone else, but I don't want to," he said.

"I don't want you to, too," I added.

"Why?" Daggers asked.

"Because I like talking to you. You're more than a caller to me. You mean much more than that," I admitted.

"You mean much more to me, too. I need to hear your voice. I need to hear that you will be okay, despite things at home," Daggers said.

"All I do is listen, Daggers, but what you've done, was help me deal with what's happening to me. I need you, too."

"Susan, I wish to God, I could talk to you outside of Sawyer House. That we could have a real relationship beyond the Center."

"I know, Daggers, but it's against policy."

"Unless I stopped calling Sawyer House," Daggers said.

"Please don't say that," I said. "I need to hear from you, too. I need to know you'll be okay." I just realized he had said the same thing to me.

Saving You Saving Me (You & Me Trilogy)

There was a small gasp on the other line, and then Daggers' voice came loud and clear. "I'll talk to you soon."

"I look forward to it," I said. "Daggers, my sweet man, how did you get such a nickname?"

"I wasn't always so sweet," Daggers said. "I had to hustle when I was growing up poor on the streets, especially after I ran away from home. I had to get tough, tough enough to send someone to the hospital, if they messed with me. One day I was sleeping on the street, and a man tried to undress me, take my clothes, and even tried to feel me up. I became so angry, I knifed him. Daggered him. He ran but didn't get far. I turned him into the police, and they sent him to the hospital. But ever since then, I toughened up. No one would mess with me, and that same attitude got me noticed by some people who helped pulled me off the streets, get cleaned up, get educated, and have shelter. I went and got a tattoo of a dagger on my shoulder and wore it proudly. That's how I became Daggers," he said.

*****

I arrived home late after talking to Daggers, my heart twisted in sadness for him, and thinking how it took a lot of courage for some big guy like Daggers to call and admit to having such a messed up addiction.

After showering and doing some homework, I crawled into bed and was out in seconds.

*****

I dreamt of thick muscular arms holding me, while a handsome face nuzzled against mine, kissing me with dove soft lips. "You're my light, my hope," he was saying as he kissed my eyelids, my cheeks and lips before plunging his tongue in to taste mine. His tongue was honey sweet, and I couldn't get enough of his kisses.

My hands roamed his smooth muscular bare back as he pressed his hips close to mine.

"Say it," he demanded. "What do you want?"

"I want to feel you…"

"Where?"

"All over."

"Tell me what to do."

"Keep doing what you're doing," he said, setting up a video camera. I grabbed the camera and began filming him as he undressed. Then I kissed him on his muscular bare chest.

He moaned against me, kissing my jawline and licking my neck. His fingers traced the skin on my back, softly while I explored the large expanse of his chest, torso, and hips. He lifted me until I was straddling his waist with my legs wrapped firmly around, and he had plunged his face into the crevices between my chest, kissing it with soft light kisses. I was wearing my navy pleated miniskirt with my hearts underwear and it flew up to my waist, exposing my underwear. He chuckled, seeing the hearts on my underwear and proceeded to gently slide them off after kissing the area covered by a few of the hearts. "Hmmm," he growled, "hearts strategically placed can drive a man crazy." Lost in the sensation his kisses were having on me, the back of my mind asked where had I heard that before. Then I remembered – Collins McGregor had said that.

"I can't get enough of you," he said in his sexy velvety voice that sent shudders down my spine, between kisses. "I've waited for you for so long, and now you're mine."

******

I woke up from my naughty dream of what I felt I was having with Daggers or was it Collins McGregor? I was getting both of them confused with each other. While I lusted after Collins McGregor, I believed I loved Daggers. This was a revelation for me. I knew I could not be with Daggers in reality, but with Collins McGregor, I actually had a chance for a real relationship…if I agreed to what he wanted out of the relationship. Whatever it was, I was affected by both, with my body quivering, and my heart racing, both men had an immediate physical and psychological effect on me which I could not shake. Lola was grinning like a cat, while Serious Susan was fanning herself with her hands.

What was I doing dreaming of Daggers? He seemed so right for me in the dreams, but now awake, he seemed like the last person on earth I should get involved with.

I crawled out of bed, putting a robe over my t-shirt and shorts before I headed out of my room and to the kitchen. I got my glass out of the cupboard, poured bottled water into it, and headed back to my room.

The voices were loud. Mom and Dad's raised voices arguing in their bedroom. I wished to God I could drown out their voices, but I couldn't avoid it if I wanted to go back to my room.

"How many more times?" Mom was shouting.

"I should ask you the same thing," Dad said calmly but with steel resolve.

"I don't care if you're the Pastor, I'm sick and tired of pretending nothing is wrong."

"If you stop drinking and seek help for your alcoholism, I wouldn't do what I'm doing."

"What I do shouldn't be the reason for you sneaking behind my back all these years. You are such a hypocrite, Samuel Sullivan. If only you practiced what you preach."

"I only married you because you claimed the baby was mine," Dad said.

"She is," Mom said, now with tears. "Can't you believe it after all these years?"

"She looks like you," Dad said, "She even acted like you when she was with the Billy kid, letting him feel her up and... I don't even want to think what he was doing with her!" Dad said. "If it wasn't for my discipline, Ann, she would be a two-bit whore like you were."

I froze, as Dad's harsh words hit my chest with such force I felt my heart being torn out of me. My Dad didn't think I was his child. My Dad didn't want me. He had only married Mom because he thought I was his. Wasn't I?

I had blocked everything about the Billy Incident since that day, the worst day of my shame. The day I shamed our family in the community. Made Dad almost lose his job because I was caught fooling around with Billy.

I was the reason behind Mom and Dad's horrible marriage. I was the reason they were so unhappy. Well, I wasn't going to be anymore. I was eighteen and now legally an adult.

I went to my closet and pulled out a large suitcase, filled it with clothes, shoes, my books, stuff animals, and diary. I grabbed my phone, backpack, and laptop and walked out of my room.

Mom and Dad were still at it, while I took a peek into Nydia's room at the other end of the house. Fortunately, she was fast asleep so she didn't hear Mom and Dad arguing. I couldn't bear to look at her and not cry.

Saving You Saving Me (You & Me Trilogy)

I told myself Nydia should be alright living with Mom and Dad. She was his for sure, even looking very much like him, while I was Mom's with an uncertain father.

Looking at sweet Nydia sleep, with her teddy bear clutched in her arms, her "baby" as she called the worn out toy, I swore that I would come back to take care of her if things between Mom and Dad got worse. But right now, she was alright. I knew for a fact Dad loved Nydia, who was always his favorite, and Mom would protect her no matter what.

I knew for a fact Mom would take care of her as best she could, because as drunk as Mom ever got, she always remembered to have fresh milk in the refrigerator for Nydia.

Chapter 13

Friday

I was standing in front of the large black gates talking into the intercom, hoping to make sense to the woman who had answered. I couldn't remember her name, but I think she was Collins' housekeeper.

I had texted Collins McGregor that I was coming to see him before driving up the winding path up the coastline to the Newport Coast and then up a few more winding paths to the front of Collins McGregor's gate.

My phone began ringing a Katy Perry ringtone, and I picked up.

"Sam," Collins McGregor's warm voice said softly. "Where are you?"

"Standing in front of your gate, trying to make your housekeeper understand I know who you are."

Saving You Saving Me (You & Me Trilogy)

Collins McGregor chuckled. "Still the same Sam. I'm going to come down and get you. Hold on a sec, I'm getting dressed."

"Don't bother," I said. "I'm only wearing my robe."

"And nothing else?" he asked smiling.

"Is that what you're wearing?" I asked.

"Less," he said.

"Oh," I said as blood rushed to my ears. "Then by all means get dressed. What would your neighbors think?"

Collins McGregor laughed. "I don't have neighbors, that's why I live way up here."

"I would say, come as you are, but what would your staff say if they saw you in the buff?"

"They would probably laugh," Collins said. "The ones who live with me have probably seen everything by now."

"Oh," I said again, thinking I was making a habit of saying it. I waited a few minutes, standing outside instead of waiting in the car. I shivered in the early morning air, as a cold wind from the ocean blew through. "It's so cold up here," I said into the phone.

"Then I'll be happy to warm you up," a voice said next to me. I jumped as Collins McGregor's arms enclosed around me, pulling me in against his chest. I should have protested, but when he touched me, all the pent up emotions and lust came spilling out of me. Instantly, I felt that electrifying heat surge between us, as white hot passion took over. His lips were immediately on mine as he thoroughly kissed me. We were standing there kissing for a while before he pulled back to whisper in my ears, his warm breath tickling them and sending a delicious thrill through me. "I miss biting these lips," he said, taking my lower lips into his and nipping on the flesh gently but enough to make me moan. I was now looking into his icy blue eyes with my eyes half-closed. "If you keep staring at me like that, Sam, I won't be able to keep my hands off you."

"Then let's head inside," I said.

"Keys?" he opened his palms out for me to hand over my keys. He took a look at my old blue Honda Civic before he opened the door to the passenger side, closed it when I got in and then went to the driver's side. "I haven't driven one of these for years," he said, turning on the ignition.

"Then enjoy it while you can," I said grinning.

Saving You Saving Me (You & Me Trilogy)

He leaned over and gave me a quick kiss before driving through the gates and into the back of the house where one of the garage doors to his ten-car garage was opened. "I don't care if it's only 3 in the morning, Sam, I'm glad you called me."

"I am, too," I said meeting his intense gaze.

He reached out to lead me into the house and into his room.

I remembered it as it was the first time I came into Collins' room. Spacious, elegant, and beautiful like Collins was.

He sat me in his armchair before heading off to the kitchen. The sounds of slamming cupboards, coffee beans being ground up, and the smell of freshly brewed coffee woke me up even before Collins placed a cup of coffee in front of me. "Drink," he said. "You feel like a popsicle, a delectable one, though, but you're cold, and I don't want you to get sick. This will warm you up."

I took a sip, and was rewarded with very good rich coffee. "You made this yourself?"

"Yes," Collins smiled shyly, which took my breath away. I haven't seen him for days, I had almost forgotten how handsome he was. "You act like that's hard to believe."

"Well, you tend to have and own a lot of things," I said quietly. "And you're Collins McGregor."

He came over to me, took the cup of coffee and placed it on the table to the side. He pulled me into his arms while using his hands to warm my arms. "And you're Samantha Sullivan," he said simply. "Just because I have a lot of money doesn't mean I'm any more or any less of a person than anyone, Sam." He smiled. "Besides, Mrs. Anderson hates being disturbed at this time of day. You witnessed firsthand how she gets."

I laughed. "You got yourself a battle axe for a housekeeper."

"That's what you get for hiring your godmother's best friend."

My eyes flew wide open, and I clapped a hand to my mouth.

Collins laughed. "You know you look so adorable like that in your fluffy robe, looking so surprised." He removed my hand from my mouth and bent down. His lips were instantly on mine while his tongue slipped in to graze the tips of my teeth. When it lightly touched mine, it was as though lightning shot between us.

My breath quickened and I suddenly wanted Collins to throw me on his bed. "Collins," I whispered, looking up at him with innocent eyes. "I want more…"

Collins gasped against me, and he pulled away gently, while his hands remained on other side of my face. His thumb traced the bottom of my lips while he said, "I want to give you more, Sam, believe me, I do, but I don't want to hurt you. I don't want to rush into things."

I involuntarily shuddered with the effects his thumb was having on my lips. He took my hands and kissed each knuckle. Without taking his eyes off of mine, he lifted me and carried me to his bed. Still gazing down intently into my eyes, he shifted aside the cream cotton duvet on his bed and gently placed me on top of the bed.

I waited anxiously for him while he lowered his head to kiss me once more on my lips and then the tip of my nose. "You must be tired, Sam." He took off his robe, revealing soft black pajama bottoms that skimmed the bones of his hips and a bare tanned muscular chest and torso. I gulped. Collins McGregor had the body of a Greek god. On his chest was a tattoo of a black heart and angel wings.

Collins smiled, noticing how I watched him. "Enjoying the view?"

"What do you think?" I asked drily, blushing a little.

"Good," he said, walking over to his dresser and pulling out a soft grey t-shirt and slipping it on.

He went over to turn off the lights and slipped into bed next to me.

Suddenly all I could feel was Collins in back of me, facing my back. He put his left arm over me and pulled me to him and kissed the back of my neck. "Now go to sleep."

Chapter 14

I awoke to a room that was as big as my parents' entire house. The bed I was in felt like clouds, and the sheets around me were fragranced with a light clean linen smell. I turned around and was face to face with perfect high cheekbones, smooth lightly tanned skin, sensuous full lips, and icy blue eyes that regarded me with amusement.

"It's time you woke up, sleeping beauty," he said, reaching over to take my hand and gently kissing my fingertips.

I removed my hand from his lips and got up. "Did we, um…"

Collins' eyebrows lifted. "If we did, you would remember."

"Did I have anything to drink?" I paced around.

"From what I remember… yes," Collins smiled. "Coffee."

Kailin Gow

"Then how did I end up in bed with you?" I asked embarrassed at first but more frustrated than anything.

"I put you in bed," Collins said. "Then you were out like a light." He sat up, and all I can see were the muscles rippling underneath his shirt and the way his pajama pants were hanging on his hips. Lola was making a sign with her fingers indicating he was scorching hot. Serious Susan was trying to look busy at first but ended up taking all of Collins in.

I kept staring at him.

He got out of bed and came over to me, putting his hands on my shoulders. His expression went from amused to concern. "Oh, baby, you're trembling like a leaf." He pulled me to him and held me tightly. "Is it because you thought something happened between us? We both wanted to, but we didn't. Nothing happened, I swear."

"What was I thinking?" I whispered so close to his chest, my head facing down.

"Don't you remember? You texted me early this morning about wanting to come see me. You didn't give any details in the text, but when you got here, we..." his mouth turned up into a smile, "kissed a lot, but we didn't do anything."

"Why not?" I asked blushing. I was relieved but disappointed at the same time, and I hated my mixed reaction.

"Trust me, Sam, I wanted to," Collins' eyes grew darker and more intense. "I wanted to so badly, but it was the first time we've seen each other for weeks, and you haven't given me an answer on the pledge."

I swallowed, remembering why I had driven over. My parents had a fight last night, and I heard my father accuse my mother of sleeping around before I was born and that he didn't think I was his baby. All the realization of why he treated me the way he did and his hang-ups about me kissing or dating a boy, made sense. The Billy Incident when I was 13 had scared him so much that he believed I would turn into a "whore" as he called my mother.

"My father…" I began.

"What baby?" Collins said, pulling me in closer.

"My father never wanted me," I said. "He never wanted to marry my mother except that he thought I was his, but he always had doubts."

"Oh baby, I'm sorry," Collins said, kissing my temple and my cheeks.

"That's why their marriage sucked so badly. That's why my mother drank herself drunk all the time." I looked up at Collins, guilt etched all over my face. I stopped myself, my eyes widened, and the feeling of shame washed over me. I had spilled my family's secrets to someone else, to Collins McGregor. Not only that, but I had driven to see him because I wanted to spite my father. I wanted to rub it into his face that I was going to sleep with someone worldly, someone who had probably had hundreds of partners, someone who would probably toss me aside once he got tired of me, someone like Collins McGregor.

"Samantha," Collins said gently, "it's not your fault. You can't blame yourself for the actions of your parents."

"Collins, I didn't mean to tell you all that," I said.

"Sam," Collins said, leading me over to the bed to sit down. "Come here," he tugged at me until I was sitting on his lap. He raised my chin with his finger so I could look at his icy blue eyes. "I know why you're here." His eyes flashed anger, but he said, "I'm not happy with how I can be used to get back at your parents. I should be angry at that, Sam. But I'm not. For some reason, my wanting to see you mattered more than how I felt about me." He took a deep breath. "I missed you, Sam. When you left, all I could think about was how could I get you back? How could I keep seeing you?"

I tried looking down, but he held my face in place as we looked at each other. "Collins, I didn't mean to…I wanted to see you," I sighed, and then my lips began trembling as I let a tear fall down my cheek. "It's been hard walking away from you. I wanted to call you, I wanted to see you again, but I couldn't." I continued. "The first day when I left, I could barely get up from bed. If it wasn't for my work, I wouldn't be able to function." My lips were quivering now, and he took his thumb to gently stroke them.

"I'm sorry," dropping his hand from my face and pulling me in so my head was lying on his chest. His hand reached up to play with my hair, stroking it gently. "I was afraid that would happen. I was going too fast, and you're so innocent."

I shook my head. "No, Collins, that wasn't it."

"Then what is it?"

I began trembling as I thought about telling him what it was. It was something I couldn't remember, something that had frightened me so much that I had unconsciously blocked it out.

"It's okay, baby," Collins held me close again. "You don't have to tell me." He kissed my forehead, my nose, and then my lips, while stroking my back. Collins was so sweet, so gentle with me.

I looked up into his warm icy blue eyes and leaned in, gently kissing his bottom lip and then his top lip. He closed his eyes, and I pulled his face closer as I kissed him harder, more passionately.

He groaned and kissed me back, before he pulled away. "Sam," he said, jumping up. "I can't hold back if you keep doing this."

I tilted my head and raised my eyebrows at him, "Do what?" I asked him, suddenly thirsty. Before my tongue could shoot out to lick my lips, he was already kissing me, pushing me down on the bed, and raising my hands out above me, entwining his fingers in mine.

"God, you're so sexy," he said, kissing my jawline down to my cleavage where he had now began blowing on my skin, sending tingles up and down my spine. "I want to take you out tonight," he said. "What are you planning to do? Stay with your parents?"

"I can't go back," I said. "I'm so mad at them."

"Technically, you should go back," Collins said. "Your mother would be worried."

"She'll be too drunk to notice I'm gone," I said. I got up off the bed and stood up. "I'm eighteen now, Collins, and I've always been more of an adult than my mother."

"You should at least let her know where you are," Collins said. "I don't want anyone thinking I kidnapped you." He walked over to where my phone was, picked it up, and handed it to me. "At least text her."

I called and got her voicemail. "Mom, it's me. If you're wondering where I am, I'm at Collins' house. Talking." I ended the call and looked up. "Satisfied?"

"Sorta," he said, pulling me to him to lay a kiss on the top of my head. "I won't ever be satisfied until you're with me, Sam."

"I still haven't signed the pledge," I made a face at him, "I don't see why there needs to be one like in other normal relationships."

"That's because of who and what I am," Collins said calmly. "I take risks all the time, Sam, calculated risks. That's the way I am in everything. That's how I got to be where I am today," he walked over to his closet near the bathroom. I followed him. "Why do dating services have people fill out applications and preferences? So it's the best chance for them to find a person who fit them." He pulled off his shirt, and walked over to pick out a pale blue shirt. I watched him, riveted to his tanned, toned body. Oh, how he fits each of my preferences. Lola nodded, while Serious Susan took notes.

He turned and I was facing his well-defined sculpted back. As he slid one arm through the sleeves of the shirt and the other, I noticed a small tattoo on his right shoulder…a beautifully intricate one of an ancient-looking warrior's knife. He looked over, and smiled. "This is where I say please turn around."

I smiled back, feeling bold. "And deny me a vision I want to carry with me all day through classes and work? Never."

He smiled sweetly, showing me that little boy with angelic curly blonde hair and icy pale blue eyes, "Not today, Sam." He twirled his fingers, indicating for me to turn around. "You should get dressed."

I walked out of the closet, out of his bedroom and into the living room looking for my suitcase.

"Hi Miss Sullivan, I'm Mrs. Anderson," a woman in her fifties with strawberry blonde hair and wearing a white shirt and black skirt approached me. "Would you care for breakfast?"

My stomach rumbled in response.

She smiled, "I take that as a 'yes'." She set a plate of fruit and a fluffy croissant, cheese, and ham sandwich in front of me, along with a large glass of orange juice. I took a bite of the sandwich and ate appreciatively.

"This is delicious," I said, enjoying the lightness of the croissant and the tangy sweet and salty flavors of the smoked ham and rich cheese. I took another bite, as Mrs. Anderson placed a napkin on the table.

"Good morning, Mrs. Anderson," Collins said, sliding into the seat next to me, dressed in a navy suit and a royal blue silk textured tie. He was dashingly handsome, and reminded me of the first time I met him, at school.

"You look nice," I said, smiling at him, and feeling a strange pride that I was the girl he wanted a relationship with.

"And you're not dressed yet," Collins said. "You don't have much time or you'll be late." I rolled my eyes at him, he was so bossy. "Miss Sullivan…" Oh, is it Miss Sullivan again? "Eat up and go get dressed. I believe Mrs. Anderson's already set your clothes up in the closet."

"Closet? Yours?" I asked.

"Sam," Collins said. "We're not going to share a bedroom. You'll be sleeping in the guest room."

I must have looked disappointed because he reached over and touched my hand. "As much as I would like to have you in my room with me all the time, I expect you would want your own space, too. Now eat up and get dressed." He got up after gulping down his breakfast and draining his glass of orange juice. "I'll meet you back here when you're dressed and ready to go," he said, heading off to another part of the house.

I quickly gulped down the rest of my sandwich, left the fruit, and drank half of my glass of orange juice. Then I got up from my seat and had Mrs. Anderson lead me to the guest room. My breath caught in my throat as I glanced at the unobstructed view of the ocean's blue waves crashing against the cliffs.

"Your clothes are in the closet," Mrs. Anderson said. "I hope you don't mind me going through your suitcase to set up your clothes."

"Not at all," I said.

"You're very young," Mrs. Anderson said. "I know Mr. McGregor is very taken by you. When you left on Sunday the first time you visited, he was very upset. He may seem strong and confident on the outside, Miss Sullivan, but he's vulnerable, especially when it comes to women. He has to set up walls, barriers against them, even imaginary ones. I hope you will be patient with him…he's a good man and deserves a lot of love. He's only 24, but he's already been through more than anyone cared to."

"Thank you," I said. "I do care for him, and I want to know everything about him."

Mrs. Anderson smiled. "I was his godmother's best friend until she died recently. She was his rock. And he took her death rather hard. He doesn't have many people he can trust, Miss Sullivan. But when he does, he's fiercely protective." Mrs. Anderson looked at her watch. "I believe you have to get dressed before he marches in here to dress you himself." She smiled and left the room.

When I entered the closet, after wresting myself from that breathtaking view, I felt as though I had stepped into a high-end boutique store. There were dresses, shoes, handbags, and coats neatly hung up in the closet. My own measly clothes were hanging on one side of the closet. I quickly chose jeans, a royal blue chiffon blouse, and a black jacket. I got ready in less than ten minutes and headed out to meet Collins in the living room.

He was on the phone when I saw him. "Yes, George, that's great news. He'll be out earlier than I expected. I'll come by this afternoon to sign some paperwork. I'll see you later."

I walked over to him and surprised him by hugging him and kissing him on the lips. "That's for letting me stay here this morning."

"I want you to stay here," he said, softly. "More than you know."

Chapter 15

Friday

I drove to school in my Honda Civic, even after Collins put up a fight about wanting to drive me to school.

"I'll need it to go to the Teen Center right after school," I finally said.

He didn't argue then, instead, he encouraged it, saying he thought what I did there was incredibly important.

I spent the majority of my class drifting through school, daydreaming about Collins. He made me feel incredible, beautiful, and wanted. It was the right kind of therapy I needed right after hearing how my father didn't want me.

"Samantha?" I heard a woman's voice as I walked down the hallway to my next class.

I turned around to see Dr. Green walking towards me. "How is Sawyer House going?" she asked without any preamble.

"I really enjoy it, Dr. Green."

"I got a call from Gail, and she's practically raving about you. You made quite an impression on her. She's recommending you for a scholarship they help sponsor."

"No way," I said, my mouth opened to scream.

Dr. Green smiled and said, "It's supposed to be a surprise, but I wanted you to know in case you have second thoughts about volunteering there."

"No, no second thoughts," I said. "I love it there!"

"Good," Dr. Green said, "Looks like they just got a generous donation from a benefactor, so they can continue operations for a good long time." Dr. Green shuffled some papers in her hands, and said, "I have to run, but let me know how it turns out."

I rolled my eyes as I thought about what Dr. Green meant. Sawyer House received a major donation, and now I'm also getting a scholarship from Sawyer House. My phone began ringing to Taylor Swift. "Hi," I said.

Saving You Saving Me (You & Me Trilogy)

"Hello Beautiful," he said breathlessly and warm. "You were the most beguiling creature I've ever kissed several times this morning." He paused. "I wish it could be every morning, though."

"I'm still debating on that," I said. "Collins, I feel like a princess with you, and I love that you treat me so well."

"I want to take care of you," Collins said. "You deserve to be treated with love and respect, baby, no matter who wanted or didn't want you when you were born."

My heart melted as I listened to his words. "Collins, you didn't have to give Sawyer House a generous donation because I'm there," I said.

"Oh you think it's because you're there?" Collins teased.

"Yes," I shot back. "You would do such a thing, Collins, because you are so kind-hearted."

"What made you think I donated a large sum of hard-earned cash to an organization like Sawyer House?"

"Because you can, Collins, and because you care."

"Sam, this may sound like a shock to you, but I did not make a generous donation to Sawyer House because you work there."

"Alright I believe you," I said. If not Collins, then who could it be?

****

After school, I rushed over to Sawyer House. Gail was just leaving for the day as I walked in. "Derek's baked another plate of chocolate chip cookies for you, Sam," she said. "Lucky girl!"

"Lucky because Derek baked the cookies or because I get to eat those cookies?" I joked.

"Both," Gail said. "They're both special. Derek's like a son to me," she said, her eyes glistening. I knew Gail had lost her son Sawyer ten years ago, but it would still be painful.

"You've done wonders for Sawyer House," I said. "Dr. Green told me you'll have many more years to operate."

"Thanks to a mysterious benefactor," she said, "who donated generously."

"They didn't leave their name?" I asked, a little aggravated.

Saving You Saving Me (You & Me Trilogy)

"No, they wanted to remain anonymous ."

"Maybe it's one of the callers," I suggested.

Gail laughed. "That would be wonderful …now go out there and charm them enough to make more donations like this one. I have to run, but next time you come in, let's have a meeting. I want to see how everything is with you."

"Sure, Gail," I said while she walked away to the parking lot.

I headed for the break room to grab a bottle of water and found Derek, talking to a pretty red head I haven't seen before. She looked like a college student with her UC Irvine sweatshirt and comfortable plaid shorts and sneakers. Her red hair was tied back into a ponytail, and her blue eyes were glued to Derek's, while she nodded and smiled at everything Derek said.

As soon as I walked in, Derek turned his head from the girl and came over to me. "Hey Sam," he said putting his hand on my shoulder to lead me over to the girl. "This is Megan Newman. She's in one of my Psych classes, and another peer counselor."

"Hi," she said cheerfully, "Derek's told me a lot about you."

I looked over at him, while he grinned back at me. "All good I hope," I laughed.

"Derek? He's a good guy," Megan said. "He wouldn't bad-mouth anyone even if his life depended on it."

"So you've known each other for a while?" I asked.

Derek let go of my shoulder and said, "We dated the first semester of freshmen year. Now we're just friends."

From the look on Megan's face, it didn't seem like it, I almost said. Boy, wouldn't that be complicated to work at the same place now?

Megan nodded, "Yes, good friends. Derek's helped me see a lot of things about myself that I wouldn't have known were there." She glanced over at the round black clock hanging on the wall and got up. "My shift," she said. "I should volunteer more, because I love doing this. I love the rush this gives me, you know…but with Sorority and college work, I can only do this twice a month," she said to me. "You're lucky you and Derek get to do this a lot more." She extended a hand and shook mine, saying, "Sam, it was nice to meet you. Derek's quite impressed by you, and I can see why." She gave me a once over and walked away.

I turned around to look at Derek, my eyebrows raised. "What did she mean by that?" I asked.

Derek had the decency to blush. "I told her about you, that's all," he said. "I mentioned you were very pretty and it can be a distraction for me…"

"Derek!" I said. "That's not what I'm here for…"

Derek put out his hands, palms up, as in a hold on motion. "No, that's not what I was saying. I told her you have the knack for this, and that you're smart and mature, but so darn beautiful, it can be a distraction from everything else."

I blushed. "Derek, I don't know what to say to that, it's sweet but at the same time, ah disturbing," I laughed. "Now tell me why is a girl you once dated working here on again and off again? I'd find that more of a distraction for you than anything else."

"Oh, Megan, she genuinely loves doing this," he said.

"But she still has feelings for you, right? I can see she still likes you," I said smiling.

Derek took my hand in his and said, "You're more of a distraction for me than anything else, Sam. I can't believe you're not taken, that you don't have a boyfriend. Something's holding you back, and it's intriguing me like heck."

I pulled my hand gently out of his and said, "No, this isn't about me, Derek. Don't try to change the topic. Megan likes you and you're both working here. I don't mind, but if you're going to flirt with me, just don't do it in front of Megan, okay."

"Sam," Derek said, looking hurt. "Megan and I are just friends and that's all it's going to be. She's with someone else now." Derek looked down and up again. I couldn't tell if he was in pain or amused. He was smiling. "She's now with Jenny, her roommate," Derek said.

I nodded. "Oh, okay, now I know what she meant." I had to laugh.

Derek put his arm around me then. "I meant everything I said, though, you are a distraction." He looked at me intently then, as though he wanted to say something, but I walked out from under his arm.

"Derek," I said, "I think you're great, but…"

"I know, Sam," Derek said before I can continue. "I won't push it. You're dealing with something, and you'll tell me if you want to or when you're ready." He smiled weakly. "For now, I'll be happy to be a friend who brings you chocolate chip cookies just to see you smile."

"Oh, Derek," I said putting my arms around his neck and hugging him. "You're so sweet," I kissed his cheeks chastely, just as Megan walked in.

Derek had placed his arms around my waist, and he looked down at me with adoring eyes.

"Uh, just coming through to get myself some Red Bull," she said. She shot Derek a look that was either annoyance or relief. "Carry on, lovebirds," she said, after grabbing a can. She turned to me then and smiled. "Glad to see Derek with someone with some class," she snorted.

I pulled away from him immediately and walked to the door. "Derek, I don't know what you told her about us, but I think she's got the wrong message."

Derek looked hurt then. "Sam, I'm sorry if that looked like something else to her, but in a sense, I'm glad she does think we're together."

"Why?" I asked.

"I don't want her to feel guilty, not anymore." Derek said quietly. "When she found out she loved Jenny, instead of me, she broke my heart. She was so confused, and I was so confused. We went through a lot together because of it." Derek looked earnestly at me. "Megan and I are good friends, but I know she feels guilty about what happened in our freshman year. Sometimes I think she's here to try to make it up to me, so I'm hoping she could let go of that guilt."

"So seeing you happy with another girl will help her move on?" I asked.

"Not that I'm asking you to be that girl, but yes, it'll help her move on and stop feeling so guilty about me."

"Oh, Derek," I cried, "You're more complicated than the Callers, you know that?"

"Is it possible for Megan to see us flirting, at least?" Derek asked. "I know I sound like a desperate nut saying this, but she kind of needs closure. This guilt is eating into her relationship with Jenny."

I shook my head and crossed my arms. "Derek, if I didn't think I know you, I'd say you did this on purpose."

"Honestly, I didn't," he said wide-eyed. "Just when she's here. Please."

"No," I muttered. "I won't do it."

"It's for Megan please."

"This is a bad idea…"

"Only this once," Derek said, giving me his best lovable pathetic but cute look.

"Alright, it doesn't mean we are, though."

"No," he said, "It doesn't."

"Well, I'm going to work. I'm hoping to leave earlier today," I smiled, thinking of Collins, and his plans of taking me out to dinner.

Derek's eyes flashed before he said, "What time were you planning on leaving?"

"6 o' clock," I checked the break room clock. "It's 4 so I don't have much time."

"I'll sit in with you," Derek said moving towards me to put his hand on my shoulders. We walked past Megan, and he slipped his hand around my waist, pulling me close to him. I rolled my eyes as he grinned down at me, making our way to our desks.

There was a green light flashing when I sat down, putting on my headset and pressing the call button.

"Hi, you've reached Sawyer House, what do you want to talk about today?"

"I'm calling because a group of my friends are pressuring me to go along with something I don't want to do," a girl's voice said.

"If you don't feel comfortable doing this, what would happen?" I asked.

"They would call me a loser and stop being my friends."

"Do you want to be friends with people who want to pressure you into something you don't want, or do you want friends who are supportive of things you do want?" I asked.

"I didn't think of it that way," the Caller said.

"Mind if I ask how old are you?" I asked. Derek looked over at me, with his eyebrows raised. It was a personal question of the Caller, and the Center's policy was to try to avoid personal questions if necessary.

"I'm fifteen," the girl said.

"So you're old enough to think for yourself. In other words, you're not a baby anymore and don't need hand-holding," I said.

Saving You Saving Me (You & Me Trilogy)

"I'm not a baby," the girl said, sounding offended.

"What is it that your friends want you to do, and if you don't go along with it, what would happen?"

There was silence at the other end of the phone, and I looked over at Derek, who was watching me, his eyes glued to my lips.

Megan walked by then, and suddenly Derek was standing behind my chair, his arms leaned down to hold me while his lips bent to nuzzle my neck, his breath warm against my skin. He kissed my neck and then the top of my collarbones, while the Caller began talking. "They want me to smoke marijuana with them."

"And if you don't?" I asked.

"They will stop being my friends."

I glanced over to my right and could see out the corner of my eyes, the outline of Megan standing there, watching Derek and I. Oh my goodness. I was mad. Mad at Derek for doing what he was doing, and mad at me for going along with it just because I couldn't say no to helping people. What was I thinking?

Lola was grinning widely, while Serious Susan was shaking her head.

Kailin Gow

Worse, was that Derek's kissing my neck and shoulders was beginning to feel really good.

I concentrated on the Caller and what she was saying. "Look, it may seem like they're all the friends you have, but if you get pressured into doing something you don't want, you will only end up hating what you've done and feeling bad about yourself. That's worse than having so-called friends who don't want you as a friend just because you didn't do what they wanted you to."

"I've been friends with them since we were ten," she said.

"That is difficult to break friendships like that, but they're not considering what you want, if they're willing to drop you like that, too," I said.

"How old are you?" she asked me suddenly.

"I'm eighteen," I said. "I went through high school facing the same thing you did, but I grew up being different, and I didn't care what other people thought of me," I said.

"How do you not care what people think of you?"

"Because, I was sick and tired of it," I said. "All my life I've had to live up to what people expected of me," I said, "So I rebelled. I stop thinking about being what they thought I should be like, when I was thirteen."

"Is it better that you did?" the girl asked.

"Yes, it is. I feel confident about myself now more than I did before I turned thirteen."

We talked for 25 more minutes about why she did not feel confident enough to step out of her group of friends and make new friends. We talked about how it was important for her to develop her own interests outside of her group of friends, and to make friends from those interests. She was interested in games, but her friends were not, so we talked about how she could join a girl's gamer group or if there was not a group like that, how she could step out and form one. She was still hesitant about going against the wishes of her circle of friends, though.

"I'll be called a loser and no one would want to be my friend," the girl said.

"Those friends aren't worth having," I said. "If they can't accept who you are and encourage you to reach your potential, then you are better off without them. I know I'm going to sound like a grown up now, but this is the bottom line: You have your whole life ahead of you. Do you want to be controlled by what those girls think or do you want to become the person you were destined to be, much greater than what your so-called friends want you to be."

"I want to be a doctor," the girl said.

"You'll have a hard time getting into medical school if you start taking drugs," I said simply.

"I get it," the girl said. "It's hard to hear, but I get it, and you're not like this 50 year old shrink who's telling me this. You're a teen like I am. Thank you."

"Good luck and call me here if you need to," I said hanging up.

As soon as I hung up, I turned around to face Derek, who grabbed my face with his hands and moved his lips to mine. I didn't open up my mouth, although he was definitely a very good kisser.

I looked over at Megan then and she walked away.

Derek pulled away, his eyes blazing. "Don't you feel it?" he said, "the chemistry between us?"

I stepped back. He was definitely a very good kisser, and I didn't want to be distracted from what I had to say. "Derek, I know you like me, and I know we're friendly, but I don't want to lead you on. I'm not interested in a relationship like that with you. We're friends and that's how I like it. Just now…I regret playing along with you for Megan's sake."

A stricken look crossed Derek's face. "Oh God, Sam, I'm sorry. I saw Megan there, and you were looking so beautiful, I got carried away. I've been meaning to kiss you for a while, and I thought you liked me too. I did not mean to take advantage of our friendship."

"Derek," I said gently, taking his hand. He looked so sad. "I do care about you, but as a friend. When I started working here, I was in a kind of relationship that just got complicated. I'm still not over it. There are things I have to work out."

"Oh," Derek said, sounding disappointed. "I didn't know. Things make a little more sense now. I wished I knew so I could've backed off. I mean I really like you."

"I bet you say that to every girl you date, Derek the Serial Dater," I joked.

"Don't," he winced. "I'm only dating different girls right now because the girl I have my heart set on doesn't seem to want me." He stared at me for a second before he turned around.

"Derek," I said, "It's not because I don't want you, you're cute, sweet, funny, kind, sexy, and if I wasn't so confused about where I was on this relationship I'm in, I would've fallen for you."

He looked up, his eyes hopeful.

"But I think you need to tell Megan something about us," I said, pointing to where Megan had gone off to...the Conference Room. "I don't want to give her the wrong idea, Derek, please. If she has guilt issues about you and her, then you two have to talk. Are you over each other?"

"Yes, we are," Derek said.

"Well, I'm not sure about that. Just now when you were kissing me, I saw her expression, and it didn't look like she was happy for you. She looked jealous even."

"She did?" Derek asked. "That's strange, I mean I thought..."

"Exactly," I said. "Talk to her and figure out what's going on. Meanwhile, I'll handle the phones."

Derek smiled, as he touched my chin with his finger. "I'm still hurting from your rejection, Sam, but now I know the reason so that soften the blow." He laughed. "Whoever you're in this confusing relationship with, is one lucky guy."

Saving You Saving Me (You & Me Trilogy)

I put my arms around him and pushed him towards the Conference Room. Then I went to my desk. The green light was flashing on screen and on my phone. I sat down, put on my headset and pressed the button.

"Hi, you've reached Sawyer House, what do you want to talk about today?"

As soon as he said, "Susan," I knew who he was. Daggers. My heart began racing and my palms started sweating, as I remembered the sexy dream I had about him. "I've been thinking about you, Susan," he said.

"I have been thinking of you," I said softly.

"I couldn't sleep last night," Daggers said, "because I kept thinking I had to say something to you…to let you know how much your faith in me means to me."

"I'm glad," I said. "It's all you, though. I mean," I was flustered. "You're the one who had to make that change."

"But I couldn't do this without you, Susan." He sounded happy.

"Daggers," I said. "How are things going?"

"I started falling in love with the girl who I mentioned. She's like a breath of fresh air, and everything I want."

I felt a strange feeling wash over me, as he went on about this girl. I tried to fight it, but suddenly I didn't want him with her. I didn't want Daggers to find this girl.

"Susan, last night, she came to my house, and I wanted to make love to her, to videotape her, to collect her on film, but I stopped. I couldn't. I didn't want to because I was afraid of losing her. I didn't even have sex with her, although I really wanted to more than anything in the world. Because I love her, I wanted to wait for her to want me in that way. I didn't force or pressure her. Instead, I crawled into bed with her, held her, and fell asleep with her. And I never slept better than ever."

My entire body froze.

"Susan," Daggers said, "I imagine you to be very much like her...an angel. That's why I keep calling you. You're my lifeline, my agent for change. I think I can have a normal relationship with my girl if I can keep talking to you about my demons. I can't taint her with that or she won't want me."

I finally thawed, but felt numb. Serious Susan slapped me a few times on my face to get me to out of the daze. "What do you want, Daggers?"

Saving You Saving Me (You & Me Trilogy)

"I want to keep talking to you, I want to be able to call you every night to talk to you, and I don't want to wait to talk to you, like all the other Callers you deal with." Daggers sighed and then he said, "I'll pay you even."

"No," I said, closing my eyes. "That's just…"

"Are you saying 'no' that you won't talk to me outside of your work?"

"I'm not allowed to, Daggers, plus I won't do this for the money, but because I care for you. I want you to be happy."

"Ahhh," Daggers sexy voice sighed against my ears. "I tell you I'm falling for this girl, and you tell me this?" he said. "When I see her, I think of you, too, you know that?"

Somehow my heart jumped, but plummeted, too.

"I made a donation to Sawyer House," he said. "I hope that covers my time with you."

"Daggers, you didn't have to," I said.

"It's not because I have to, it's because I want to, Susan," he said. "I made some right decisions in life when I was younger that turned me into a very wealthy man, even at my young age. I've had such a hard start in life, Susan, it's made me appreciate everything I've got. You've helped me, no, you're helping me, and so I'm helping Sawyer House. In the beginning I wasn't even going to call Sawyer House. It was an accident that I called this line when I was looking for another line. And it was a risk. I don't do public talks or crisis centers. I do private therapy with overpaid psychs to the stars. This was a risk I took, all because I was lucky enough to get you on the line, to talk me into talking to you. So the donation? It's my calculated risk, Susan, to make sure you'll still be around."

Calculated risk? Where did I hear that before?

My head was spinning, and my heart was pounding so loudly that I feared my head would explode.

Lola had her hand clapped to her mouth, and Serious Susan looked on in horror.

"Collins?" I said so softly I could barely hear myself.

There was a deep intake of breath at the other end of the line before the line went dead.

Chapter 16

Derek and Megan found me quivering and shaking like a leaf curled up like a ball in the corner of the room. My head was in my arms, feeling so heavy that Derek had to lift my face up so he can talk to me. "Sam!" He enveloped me into his arms as the tremors kept coming over and over me again like waves. "What is it?" he asked. "What happened?"

Megan came over and gently touched my shoulders, "Here," she said, "drink this, it'll calm your nerves." He handed me a mug of tea that I nearly spilled since I was shaking so hard. Derek grabbed it out of my hand and gave it back to Megan.

After a while, I subsided while Derek held me. Gently he stroked my hair as I leaned into him, unable to control my shaking.

"It's okay," Derek said, rubbing my back. "You'll

be okay, Sam. You're safe. I won't let go until you're ready." As the tremors went through me, I held on tighter, and he tightened his grip on me until I was still.

Gradually my shaking stopped and I closed my eyes feeling like lead. I sunk into Derek, and he lifted me off the floor, carrying me as I dangled in his arms.

"How is she?" Megan asked.

"She stopped shaking," I heard Derek say. "I think that's good, but now she's out cold. Must be exhaustion. Sam has been in here almost every day for the past three or four weeks, like she was on a mission, hardly taking breaks, and when she did, she would be reading up on things. She said she was glad to be hearing other people's problems so she could stop thinking of her own. I didn't think it would be this bad."

"Something must be so deep within her that she doesn't even know what's going on with her," Megan suggested. "I've never seen anyone shake like that out of some kind of fear."

"I don't know what it is, but I want to help her," Derek said. "If she'll let me."

I felt Derek carrying me in his strong arms through

the hallway.

"Where are you taking her?" Megan asked.

"If you'll watch the phones tonight," Derek said calmly. "I'm taking her back to her home. I have the address from her paperwork."

"Alright," Megan said. "Go, this has shaken me up some."

"She'll be okay," Derek said again, grabbing my coat and my bag from my desk and making his way to the door. He got to the door, and had opened it before he stepped back and said, "Holy…"

"Sam?" Collins' voice asked with worry. "Why are you carrying Sam like that?"

"Who are you?" Derek demanded.

"I'm Sam's friend," Collins said. His worry replaced with calmness. "I'm taking her out to dinner," he added with a hint of possessiveness.

"She's in no state to go out to dinner with you," Derek said, some steel to his voice. "If you're a friend of hers, you'd understand."

"Then I'll take her home," said Collins. I felt his hands on my waist, as he tried to take me into his arms from Derek's.

Derek stepped back. "If you're that guy she's been seeing and has been trying to forget about this whole month, then I'm not letting you near her. I think she collapsed out of exhaustion and stress, worrying about you."

"That's why I'm here," Collins said, his voice betraying how he felt for me.

Some force in me surged up to make me cry out for him, wanting him near me. "Collins," I whispered. "Oh God, Collins…"

"Sam," Derek said, his eyes shining. "You're up. I was worried for a moment, but…"

"Can you put me down?" I asked.

"Oh yeah, sorry, I forgot I was holding you," Derek said, nearly dropping me.

I stumbled to my feet, as Collins placed his hand on my waist, steadying me as I looked up into his beautiful face. This beautiful man with the blazing adoring icy blue eyes and full lips was the poor baby boy whose mother verbally and physically abused at birth. My Mr. Collins McGregor was Daggers. My sexy Caller who craved verbal abuse was the man I couldn't get enough of.

Saving You Saving Me (You & Me Trilogy)

"Sammy," he said, "I have to talk to you." His face was in such anguish, it made me want to cry. There was so much between us that was unspoken as we stared into each other's eyes.

I looked over at Derek, whose face had turned to stone, as he watched Collins take my hand and lovingly caress it. "Derek," I said. "Thank you for helping me. I have to go, but I'll see you soon."

Derek looked down to the ground, before he turned his brown eyes to me hiding some bitterness and anger. "Yeah, I'll see you later." He glanced over at Collins with anger in his eyes, turned and walked away.

Chapter 17

We left my car in the parking lot, while I slid into the backseat with Collins. Instead of his Aston Martin, we were being driven by his driver in his black Cadillac Escalade.

I cocked my eyebrows at him and tilted my head. "What happened to the Aston?" I asked.

"At home," he said. "The state I was in before I headed here to see you, I'd have crashed the Aston." He took a deep breath and said, "I wanted to tell you, but I was so scared if you knew about me, about my need for an abusive sick relationship; I would scare you off."

"So you became Daggers?" I asked.

Saving You Saving Me (You & Me Trilogy)

"I *am* Daggers," Collins said. "That was my nickname for when I was a street punk, growing up on the fringe of gangs and drug dealers in Santa Ana. I was a walking hating disaster, always picking fights, always trying to get myself beaten senseless or killed."

I traced the outline of his face with my fingers, feeling him, touching him, not quite ready to believe the voice I had listened to was this beautiful creature before me. My Daggers was my Collins. My poor Collins...when I thought how he grew up and what he had become today, I did not think I could ever love him more than I did now.

"Sam," Collins said, "like you, I'm having a hard time wrapping my head around you being Susan from Sawyer House. I mean, in the back of my mind I knew you were Susan, but being Daggers and talking to Susan as Daggers was the only way I could tell you about my past and my sick need. I wanted to see how you would react to Dagger's dark secret. I never thought you would figure out who Daggers was nor want to get close to him because of his cravings, but you seemed so accepting of Daggers."

"Why wouldn't I be?"

"Because of the way you reacted when I showed you the sixth condition for my agreement."

"I still have a problem with it, Collins because I can't do it. Other people may have no problem with it, but I can't. Of all the things in the world, that sixth condition baffled me, made me worried about you, made me worry about what you expected of me. I could not agree to it, Collins."

Collins pulled out the paper and read me the number six condition:

6. Must be willing to be videotaped during sex.

"I will remove it from the conditions, Sam, if you want me to, but if you want to keep it, I'm fine with it. As much as I thought I had to have it in our relationship, it no longer matters."

I must had tears in my eyes, because Collins leaned in to kiss my eyelids, kissing away a tear, before kissing my lips softly. "But isn't that one of your absolute conditions? The deal breaker?"

He was looking at me with such adoration. "I'll be willing to try, for you. Don't you understand? When it comes to you, there are no deal breakers."

Saving You Saving Me (You & Me Trilogy)

I looked at him, my beautiful tortured walking hating disaster, as he called himself. He was my Daggers and my Collins rolled up in one yin/yan self-loathing/egotistical hot yet deeply disturbed package. I realized how much I cared for him, when I said, "Keep condition six."

Collins kissed my temple and asked me, "Are you sure?"

I picked up his hand and held it to my cheeks. "Collins, when will you realize whatever happens will happen in a relationship sans paperwork." I kissed the palm of his hand, and he closed his eyes. I took his hand and began kissing his fingertips. "Something happened today when I realized you were Daggers, and Daggers was you."

Collins pulled me into his lap and held me. "What?"

"I had a breakdown, Collins, my mind and body couldn't process it, it was as though I couldn't handle my intense overwhelming feeling of love and desire for you, Collins. I was falling for Daggers, but I also loved you. I fell in love with both of you, I guess - past, present, and future.

Collins' face was shrouded in mystery. He pulled me in close so my head was resting against his chest. "Is that what happened when I arrived at Sawyer House? You had a breakdown?"

He looked so worried, "I don't want to be the cause of your breakdown, Sam. I don't want you having *any* breakdowns." He looked at me seriously then. "Sam, you are the kindest, sweetest, and most loving woman I've met, and I know you would put everyone else's wants and desires over your own to your detriment. There is something that is worrying you so much, deeply buried in you about us, that caused that breakdown, isn't there? Is it your about your mother or father? I remember how you were constantly worried about what your father thought of you."

As Susan, I did tell Daggers about the pressures of growing up under my father's shadow. While looking at Collins, I had to remember he was also Daggers, who knew many things about me. Just like I knew more about Daggers than Collins.

The look on his face made my heart drop. He had doubt written all over his face. I threw my arms around him and began kissing him, wanting to erase that look of dread. My lips were on his, and when our tongues touched, all the tension and doubts we had, faded away as we were all lips, hands all over each other.

The car came to a stop and we pulled away from each other as Vincent came around back to open Collins' door.

We had been driving for a while, and it didn't occur to me where we were going until Collins said, "I promised I'd take you out to dinner tonight, so here we are."

He extended his elbow, and I looped my arm through. "Where are we?" I asked.

"The Sky Room," Collins said.

"But I'm not dressed for it," I said, looking down at my jeans and blouse and jacket.

"Don't worry, Vincent's brought along a dress and shoes for you to change into," Collins said, kissing my hand.

We took the elevator to the top of a building, and when we stepped out, we were in a restaurant with a view of the Long Beach harbor and city views. "It's breathtaking," I said.

"Not as breathtaking as you." Collins nipped my ear, and I flushed.

A handsome young man in a suit walked by then and smiled at me, his eyes lingering on my tight skinny jeans before meeting my eyes.

Collins placed his arm around my shoulder, pulling me closer to him. The young man noticed Collins, then, frowned and walked past us to the other side of the restaurant. Collins muttered, "Even in just jeans, you're the prettiest girl in this room. Maybe we can get away with wearing jeans."

"I hope so," I said.

A pretty tall and thin girl with copper hair and blue eyes, dressed in a black A-line dress came over to us with a menu. Her blue eyes devoured Collins as she took him in from head to toe. "Mr. McGregor, it is a pleasure having you dine here tonight." She smiled hungrily at Collins, while Collins took my hand in his and pressed his lips to my knuckles.

"I'm here for a special occasion," he looked adoringly at me, "Katrina made reservations for us."

The hostess glanced briefly at me, frowning at my outfit, before returning her gaze to Collins. "Well of course, Mr. McGregor." She led us past the tables and into a private room with a gorgeous view of the ocean and city night lights. She seated us and handed us menus before leaving.

Collins squeezed my hand. "Well, we bypassed having to change you into a dress, altogether."

I looked amazed at Collins. "How did you manage to bypass the dress code?"

Collins chuckled. "I own the building."

"Oh," I said. "Of course."

Collins reached over to hold my hand. "I've made some pretty good calculated risks in real estate, among other things, and have done well because of it." His icy blue eyes blazed at me. "Materially I'm considered rich, but it means nothing if I'm unhappy."

I leaned over to kiss him softly on his lips. "You deserve to be happy, Daggers."

At the name "Daggers", Collins' eyes grew dark and a look of desire flash across them. "You make me happy, Sam." He kissed me gently on the corners of my lips before kissing me fully, using his tongue to pry open my mouth to taste my tongue. The touch was electrifying, and my entire body filled with desire. I leaned in, and he grabbed the back of my head to kiss me harder on my lips, my jaws and neck.

"We're in a restaurant," I managed to say.

"In a private room with a lock on the door," Collins now Daggers hissed, getting up to turn the lock.

"You knew that?"

"I'm always prepared, honey," Daggers smiled wickedly.

"Oh you are, are you?" I teased. "That's pretty bad, you naughty boy." I leaned in to nibble his ears.

He groaned before grabbing me, and lifting me onto his lap while he pulled my head back and kissed me passionately.

I kissed back matching him in passion as his tongue tangled with mine in a delicious sensual dance. His hands had slipped under my blouse and were making their way to the back to unclasp my bra.

All of a sudden, my entire body tensed.

Collins stopped and jumped up from his seat, running his hand through his sexy ruffled dirty blonde hair, fear and trepidation replacing his look of desire. "What's happening?" he asked. "What is it, Sam? Is it something I've done?"

I closed my eyes and started taking large gulps of air and breathing through my mouth. After a minute my body relaxed.

He took a big breath and let it out slowly. "Sam," he bent down, hands on his knees, trying to catch his breath. "You've no idea how worried I was, seeing you like that." He looked earnestly into my eyes. "Promise me you get some help with it. You were paralyzed with fear, and it scares me to think I may be causing it or something I'm doing may be causing it." He sat back down to take my hands in his, kneading them, massaging my palms and fingers. "You have no idea how much I've missed you. From day one, I couldn't stop thinking about you. From day one, you've driven me crazy, and as a man who gets what I want all the time, you're something I want so badly, but couldn't have." He closed his eyes and looked tortured.

"Collins?" I asked. "What is it?"

"I'm going to take away the sixth condition. I don't want it. I want to get as far away from it as I can…not only was it bad for me, but I think, baby, it's part of the reason you're so frightened."

My face froze. I had pushed his sixth condition to the back of my mind, trying to ignore it.

"When I first presented it to you, you looked at me like I was a two-headed monster," Collins said. "It's not something I'm proud of, either. It's what I needed in a relationship with a woman because that's how my messed up mind thinks." He took a deep breath. "When you said you needed time to think about it, I knew you were going to have a problem with it. But at the time, that's all I knew about how a relationship between a man and a woman could be, Sam. I tried to leave you alone. I tried all kinds of distractions, and worked extra hard. I even went on a business trip to Seattle and Vancouver. But I couldn't stop thinking about you. And you wouldn't return my calls. You texted me a few times, but I needed to hear your voice…"

"Collins," I said, wanting to reach out to him.

"You wouldn't call me back for days and when you emailed me, it wasn't the same. I needed to hear your voice. No matter how. So I was desperate. I tried to call you at Sawyer House to talk to you there because you weren't returning my calls on your cell and at your parents' house. I needed to talk to you, Sam. I didn't realize how much until you walked out of my house that day I presented my conditions. I've always had conditions, Sam, ever since I started accumulating wealth and had been burned by a few girls I knew."

At the mention of other girls, I felt a pang of jealousy.

"It's part of my calculated risks plan. It's worked in my business life, so it should work in my personal. But when it came to you, everything went to shot. I didn't care anymore about the conditions. All I wanted was you, Sam." He ran his hand through his hair before setting adoring icy blue eyes on me.

"I didn't mean to become Daggers over the phone to you, Sam," he choked. "I had called in to find you at Sawyer House, thought you would be working in the administration area, not the call center itself. You had been avoiding my calls, and I had to talk to you, at least hear your voice to see if you were alright. When you begin talking to me, as Susan, and made me feel so comfortable about opening up, were so accepting of all the deep dark things I was telling you, I couldn't stop myself. It was like a dam that had been broken, and you were the kindest, sweetest person in the world for me to talk to, to feel like I was not this two-headed monster, but a human being."

He came over to me and bent down to take my hands in his, "I love you, Sam, and I don't want to do anything to jeopardize the love we have for each other." He reached into his pocket to pull out the paperwork and tore it in pieces. "I don't need this anymore with you. And there won't be anyone else." He kissed me ever so gently on my lips before pulling me to his chest. "All I need is you."

Chapter 18

Sunday – 1 Month Later

Another kiss – and then another. We spent hours kissing in bed every morning since Collins and I officially became a couple. At first, it came as a shock to everyone, but I couldn't be any happier, and the smile I got from Collins every morning, said he was just as happy.

There were so many changes after I moved in with Collins, against my parents' wishes. I had reservations at first about moving in with Collins so quickly, but he had agreed I would have my own room and that I could have my own space. Because he felt the need to talk to me every day and to know I was not going to have another breakdown, ways of helping each other cope with our messed up demons; moving in together was the best solution for us. Dad, who never said anything about the argument he had with Mom, barely acknowledged me since the day I moved out. The only thing he was worried about was about how his congregation would see him. Mom, on the other hand, was glad I had left home, just to be away from all the negativity.

She said when I was packing my things, "Sam baby, you're legally an adult now. You could move out, but I'll still be worried about you. It's what mothers do."

It was Sunday, and I had opened my eyes sleepily to see Collins gazing at me, with love in his eyes.

"Hi," I said, shyly, "What are you thinking?"

"How lucky I am to have you." He traced his finger on my cheeks. "I can't seem to stop touching you. Your skin is so soft and flawless." He took both of my hands, entwining his fingers through mine and lifted my arms above my head as he kissed my mouth slowly and thoroughly.

"Hmm, Mr. Hot Bod and Perfect for Me," I said sighing to myself. "Now that's how a girl gets awakened in the morning."

"Mr. Hot Bod?" Collins asked, raising his eyebrows.

Saving You Saving Me (You & Me Trilogy)

"Just something me and the girls call you," I said wriggling playfully underneath him. I grinned. My girls, Lola and Serious Susan. My id and my ego. My subconscious pleasure side and my subconscious reality side.

"You call me that?" Collins began tickling me.

I struggled underneath him, trying to avoid him from tickling me.

He shifted so his hips were straddling my hips, and his thighs tightened against mine, keeping me from moving. He started tickling me with his fingers all over my stomach until I had tears in my eyes. "Stop stop!" I cried laughing.

Collins pulled back a little while I tried to move underneath him. The harder I struggled, the tighter he held me with his thighs. "Will you stop wriggling," he groaned, "you're going to… oh screw it," he bent down and began kissing my mouth until both of us were breathless.

Then he turned over onto his back. "What you do to me, Sam…I'm supposed to be up and dressed, getting ready for a trip to Chicago, but all I want to do is tickle you and kiss you."

"I don't want you to go," I said, pouting.

He got up from the bed, wearing his soft pajama pants that clung to his firm butt in a way that made me flush. "I have to. They're letting him out, for good behavior. I have to go get him."

I gulped. "I'm sorry I can't go with you to meet your brother."

"Technically, my half-brother," Collins said. "He's going to be a handful, Sam. I think it'll be easier if I met with him first before introducing you."

He walked into the closet while I got out of bed, wearing a UC Irvine t-shirt and Collins' boxer shorts. I went to my side of the closet, pulled out a green silk halter tie dress. I pulled my t-shirt off and dropped my shorts, while slipping the dress over my head. I turned around and saw Collins standing there with a big grin on his face.

"What are you grinning at?" I asked.

"What a lucky guy I am," Collins said, slipping his arm around my waist and pulling me in for a kiss. "It's only for a few hours, but I'm going to miss you. We haven't been apart a day since you moved in, and that's how I like it, but…"

Saving You Saving Me (You & Me Trilogy)

"I can always skip lunch with my mom and work at Sawyer House and go with you," I said.

"No, you haven't seen your mom for almost a month. I know you two have things to talk about. Sawyer House – I'm proud that my beautiful girlfriend can spare time away from me to help others. It's one of the many things I love about you."

I rubbed his shoulders, massaging his back with my thumbs. "Tate'll be attending the same school as me, right? That's why you were at my school the day we met," I said.

Collins leaned into me. "I remember every detail of that day, Sam. I think I fell in love with you the moment you bumped into me and flashed me your hearts."

"Hearts?" I asked.

"The hearts on your boy-style underwear," he laughed. "I've never seen a girl wear those before, and it was so darn cute but sexy."

"It's a good thing I'm of legal age, Mister," I said, "and a consenting adult or what I'm about to do to you would have my parents calling the authorities."

"Is that a threat?" Collins said in a low voice.

I put my fingers to his lips and began rubbing his lower lip. He closed his eyes for a minute in anticipation of what I had in mind. When he opened his eye, he saw me bend down under my dress and slip off my underwear. It was the multi-hearts boy-style one I wore the first time we met. He smiled, and then I took it and tucked it neatly into the inside pocket of his jacket.

His mouth opened in astonishment, I closed it with my fingers. "That's to remind you of me," I said, "and to get you to come back as soon as you can."

His eyes were shining with amusement, love, and desire. "Having this with me all the time is going to keep me distracted all day. I can imagine what TSA will think if they find it in my jacket pocket."

"That you must be a pretty happy guy," I said kissing him.

****

Vincent drove Collins to the airport while I drove my white Honda Civic to Dad's church. I hadn't been there since finding out the truth about what he thought of me. He had said he only married Mom because she was pregnant, and he thought I was his.

Saving You Saving Me (You & Me Trilogy)

When I got there, it felt strange being in the back. Service was already underway, and Dad was standing in the pulpit, while everyone was standing in their seats singing. Mom and Nydia was sitting in front, where I was conspicuously missing.

My heart fell. Despite everything, we were still family, and I missed them more than I cared to admit. I got up from my seat in back and walked down the center aisle to take a seat next to Mom. As I walked, I felt all eyes on me. The looks I got were mixed with anger and indignation.

"Have you heard she's living with an older man out of wedlock," I heard someone whisper.

Lies! Collins wasn't an older man. He was only a few years older than me.

"They say she drove Mrs. Sullivan to drink."

I was furious now and leaned into the face of the girl who said that. "You're at church, ladies, it's not nice to gossip,"

Their mouths dropped open for a second.

"For your information, my boyfriend is only a few years older than me, and I did not drive my mother to drink."

I sat down next to Mom. She looked up, joy filling her eyes, with a tinge of sadness.

Nydia, on the other side of Mom, was beaming.

"I'd knew you would show up!" she squealed and had to be hushed.

"Of course I had to if you're here," I chuckled.

She hushed me back. My how I missed my sassy little sister.

When service ended, and everyone in our row stood up, I felt a touch on my elbow and turned around.

Young Pastor Michael was smiling at me. "Sam, good to have you back."

"Collins wanted me to go to church today," I said proudly.

Michael kept his gaze on me. "Then he seems like a bright guy."

I tilted my head and cocked my eyebrows. "Coming from you, that is quite a compliment."

"No, I mean it, Sam," Michael said. "He knew a good thing when he saw it and grabbed the opportunity before it slipped away. No wonder why he's so successful."

"You don't believe in all the gossip then, too," I said. "You're not bothered by it?"

"It's just gossip. I don't care much about it because I know you and I've met Collins. It's not a December/May kind of thing you two have. When I saw Collins leading you away that day, I knew I didn't stand a chance with you."

I reached out and squeezed his hand. "Thank you for telling me. Now we can avoid any awkwardness, right?"

"Oh, hey, of course," Michael said. "Of course. Well, I have to go lead the youth group class right now." He smiled at me, his eyes taking my face and dress in. "It was good seeing you again, Sam. Don't be a stranger," he said walking away.

"Whew," Mom said, "Now we can go have lunch."

Chapter 19

After we took Nydia to music class, I drove Mom to A Restaurant, a swanky restaurant in Newport Beach that Collins and I often go for Friday night chicken pot pies. It was the kind of restaurant that felt very grown up, and she picked up on it as soon as we entered the door.

"Very impressive, Sam," she said, taking in the rich dark tones of the restaurant furnished in red leather and woods. She looked proud, yet sad at the same time.

We ordered and while waiting for our food, Mom said, "I know I haven't been much of a mother to you, Sam, but I've always been there, watching you grow up. Now you're all grown in the way you dress, the restaurants that you choose, and staying with Collins McGregor."

"I know Mom, but you have to admit, I've always been more grown up than other kids."

Saving You Saving Me (You & Me Trilogy)

"Not really, Sam," Mom said. "You were playful, fun, and carefree as a child. When you turned thirteen, that changed. You became so serious, less sociable, and even angrier. I thought it was because you had become a teenager, but not all teens act that way. I should have been worried, but there were pluses, like you started taking homework more seriously and did not date at all."

"Mom, in a way, I wish I was more like a regular teenager, but I'm fine with who I am. I don't want you to blame yourself for how I turned out because I think I turned out alright."

"No thanks to me," Mom said.

"Mom!" I protested. "You're fine. No matter who disagrees with you, and despite your drinking problem. Despite the drinking, you're a great mom." There. I said it. Lola was clapping, and Serious Susan was clapping, too.

"Sam, I'm trying to stop drinking. Believe me, I try but it's been hard. But I've made some progress at a local Alcoholics Anonymous. I had too. For Nydia's sake. She's still little, not like you. In a way I'm glad you moved out. It wasn't until you left to stay with Collins that I realized how bad my drinking problem has become."

Kailin Gow

"Mom, I'm proud of you for trying though. Does Dad know? I know he worries about you, especially when you're drunk."

"Yes, he does, baby, your father knows about me going to AA. But it's too late. My drinking has already caused a rift between us." Mom began shaking. "He's already filed for a divorce."

I reached over and pulled my mother in for a hug. "Mom, I'm sorry. I know Dad thought you were pregnant with his baby so he felt forced to marry you and start a family in the first place."

Mom gasped and recoiled from me. "How do you know about that?"

"I heard you and Dad arguing that morning. I heard him say some hurtful things, yet I didn't know if he meant them.

"Oh baby," Mom said. "You weren't supposed to hear that. I've tried to shield you from your father's wrath. He didn't want to marry me, but did it because I was pregnant with his child, or so he thought. He never wanted it, and had already started dating another girl before he found out I was pregnant."

So it was worse than I thought.

A look of surprise came over Mom's face. "Sam I just remembered. Be sure to use birth control when you're with Collins. You can get caught up in the moment and forget."

I tensed before telling her, "Mom, Collins and I haven't done it yet," I blushed pink.

"You haven't?" she asked shocked. "But Collins must be so experienced."

"No, we haven't done it," I said, embarrassed to have this conversation with my mother, who apparently did not follow the advice she just gave me and was pregnant with me before she married Dad.

"But you've been living together all this time…"

"Mom, don't you have some faith in me for not being so stupid as to get knocked up like you?" As soon as the words came out of my mouth, I felt awful, so awful I couldn't face Mom.

Mom looked like I had slapped her. She took a sip of water before facing me, though, and said, "As you would like to believe, I did not sleep around when I became pregnant with you. I was a virgin, and the first boy who came along who showed me any attention, we had sex. And

because I was so naïve about it, and so overprotected by my
parents about sex, I didn't use any protection. I was 21
years old, and I didn't even know how to use a condom to
save my life. As naïve as I was, I thought I would know all
that when I got married and my husband would show me,
but guys expect the girl to know what to do, too. As much
as I'd like to believe the guy would take care of the
situation, it's our bodies, and we have to be the one
prepared. I wasn't so I became pregnant, and I had started
dating a boy from church about the same time who was
slow to get me to bed. We did and I told him I was
pregnant, and he believed it was his, and so we married."

I was numb.

"It didn't mean I didn't love you less just because
you weren't Samuel's daughter. In fact it made me love
you more because you were mine. My little baby girl," she
said tears glistening in her eyes.

I didn't know what to say. For the first time in all
my life, I didn't know what to say to my mother. I sat there
while Mom took another sip of her water.

Finally, I said, "I love you, too," realizing how true
that was. No matter where I came from, this crazy drunk

Saving You Saving Me (You & Me Trilogy)

messed up woman in pearls, neatly styled hair and Pastor's wife chic was my mother. I was programmed genetically and naturally to love her. Just like Daggers was programmed to love his abusive mother, no matter what.

*****

After lunch, I drove Mom back to church where she picked up Nydia from Music class. "What are you going to do about Dad wanting a divorce?"

Mom's face nearly crumbled, and I held her in my arms. Jeez, my mother had just told me I was a bastard, and that I was never Samuel Sullivan's daughter, and here I was comforting her instead of the other way around. I held her in my arms, but at the same time, I hoped to God, I was not like her, that I would not turn into her. At that moment, Dad's words to Mom that night they had the argument came back to me. "She's a whore just like you."

Chapter 20

I had to talk to someone about all the crap I was going through. It felt like I would explode with all the emotions I was feeling...anger, hurt, betrayal, sadness, guilt... I didn't want to be the strong one. I didn't want to be the one who had to tell everyone things were going to be fine. I didn't want to be the one who had to keep picking up the pieces for everyone. I could only be so strong...

I called Collins' number, but got his voicemail. He was probably in a meeting and couldn't pick up. I waited and waited. I called him again, and got his voicemail. "Hey, I miss you. How is everything? Collins, I'm feeling vulnerable right now. I wish you could be here to hold me..." I took a deep breath and tried to remain calm. "I'm just...I miss you." I hung up and drove to Sawyer House, where maybe I could focus on other people's problems so much that I could forget my own. It was what helped me through that awful time when Collins and I were apart. This was what I needed.

Finally I drove to Sawyer House and punched the number to walk in. I hadn't been there for a few weeks, mainly because of my breakdown. Gail had thought I needed some time off to rest and get over stress and exhaustion. I didn't argue with her, knowing the reason for the breakdown was because of Daggers.

"Oh hi," I said as I walked into the break room to grab a bottle of water. Derek was there finishing his drink. When he saw me, his eyes lit up, and he came over.

"Sam," his eyes perused my face. "I didn't think I'd see you back here."

"I still want to get a scholarship to Stanford, Derek…"

"But wouldn't Collins take care of that?" Derek asked, a hint of bitterness in his voice. "He could buy his way…"

I turned to Derek, "What are you saying, Derek? You don't even know him. He wouldn't want to buy…"

"He was the one who donated that large donation to Sawyer House, Sam. He got you that scholarship. Now he wants to keep you in his bed by buying you," Derek said.

"That is not true," I said. "It had nothing to do with how I feel about Collins."

"Then why are you with him?" Derek asked.

"Because he needs me, and I need him," I said simply.

Derek walked up to me and looked me in the eyes. "Tell me, is he the real reason why you had that breakdown?"

"It's not his fault," I said.

"I'm worried about you, Sam. And I'm mad as hell at him for whatever he did to make you break down like that."

"There's nothing wrong, Derek," I said weakly.

"Then why did your body shut down like that?" he said. "What is his hold on you, Sam?"

"Nothing. It's nothing he's done, Derek."

"Subconsciously you're holding back with him, Sam. There's something about him that you haven't accepted or have a hard time accepting."

"Why do you say that?"

"Because the whole time you were here trying to get him out of your head, you acted so guarded, like you had some deep dark secret. Turns out Collins was your deep dark secret."

My heart raced as I thought, could Derek know about Collins being Daggers? "Derek, I'm fine," I said.

"Tell me then," Derek moved in close, and his hands were on mine. "Why you haven't completely committed to him?"

"What do you mean?" I was fully aware of his hands on mine and how close he was standing, so close that if I moved, my face would be on his chest.

"Meaning, this," He kissed me then, a tender kiss that grew passionate as he pulled me closer. Because of my vulnerable state of mind, because God knows what, I opened my mouth, and his tongue darted in to taste mine. Derek groaned with satisfaction, before I pulled back and stepped away. "You responded to me, Sam," Derek grinned. "There's chemistry there. If you're so taken in by Collins McGregor, you wouldn't have responded, you wouldn't have all these issues – doubts, breakdowns…"

"How dare you!" I said rushing over to him, and slapping him across the face.

He grabbed my hands and pulled them down. "I'm sorry, Sam, I wanted to prove…" He pulled me into his chest and held me, while I began crying. I was happy. I was deliriously happy with Collins, so why was I crying? Why did I feel like I had to hold back?

"Do you have sex with him?" Derek asked.

"That's none of your business," I said fiercely.

"I've seen pictures of Derek with a girl always by his side. The guy's a player, and the girls he's with are no innocents like you are."

"He respects me," I said.

"He's not sleeping with you," Derek said. "Trust me, if a guy has a girl like you at his house every day… if I had you, Sam, I'd be making love to you every day, every hour." His eyes blazed with such hunger, my body began to get warmer. He reached up a finger and traced my face. "Sam, any guy would be crazy not to want all of you."

"Derek, he's got issues and I have issues…"

"Which I want to figure out," Derek said softly against my cheeks. "You know I care for you a lot, and when you broke down like that, I was so damn worried. I didn't know if you were going to come out of it. All I knew was that someone had hurt you once so badly to make you react so traumatized." Derek traced my cheeks with his fingers. "When I saw him walk in and the look on your face as soon as you saw him, I knew he had to be the reason. And all I wanted was to punch him out for making you react like that."

"Do you want to punch me out now?" a voice came from the doorway of the break room. Collins stood there, his face seething with steel fury hidden underneath. "Get your hands off my girlfriend or I will walk over there and make sure you never walk again."

Derek jumped away from me, and I closed my eyes. "Collins..." He was looking at me with hurt, anger, and love in his icy blue eyes. "Derek was just worried about me, that's all."

"And he couldn't keep his hands off you too?" Collins asked, crossing his arms. "I got your message and was so worried that I dropped everything to get back to you. The crew for my private jet was not prepared to take off last minute like that, but we made the best of it, getting here earlier than we expected. I traced your phone to here, just to find you in the arms of another man." He gestured at Derek in disgust.

I ran over to Collins then. I grabbed hold of him and tried to put my arms around him. "Collins, I'm sorry..."

Kailin Gow

He pointed a finger at Derek. "I heard what you said to my girlfriend about me, and I want to be clear about this. She's my girlfriend, and if she has any issues with me, she should be addressing it with me rather than you."

His face still masked in fury, Collins placed his arms around me and pulled me into him to kiss me hard, lifting me to slide my entire body against his so that my legs had to wrap around his waist, straddling his hips. He pushed me unto the wall and began taking off his jacket. "Mr. Psych there thinks I don't desire you enough to make love to you 24 hours every day, we'll see about that."

With my legs wrapped around Collins' waist, and my face buried in his hair, I glanced over at Derek, who was fixated in his place, watching us, as Collins began unbuttoning my shirt until all I was wearing on top was my black lace bra. Derek's eyes caught mine, and he had a look of anger mixed with desire. He shook his head, bunched his hands into fists and walked out, not looking at either of us.

I raised my hands and was about to slap Collins when he caught my wrist midair. I was so mad that I tried wrenching it free. "That was cruel, Collins," I said. "You didn't have to do this in front of Derek. He just wanted to help me."

"He wanted to get into your pants anyway he knew how," Collins said.

Anger flashed in my eyes as I looked at Collins. "He's a friend, and he's right about some things. I know how he feels about me, and this? This is cruel, mean, and…" I raised my hand again.

His eyes grew darker and his lips curled into a sensual wicked grin. "So you want to play?" he said. "It's about time."

He lifted me and flipped me over his shoulders, walked to the break room table, grabbed my purse, and carried me out of Sawyer House out to the parking lot where his black Escalade SUV was parked in front of the building. Vincent was sitting in front when Collins opened the back seat door and sat me down, buckling my seat belt in place while he clamored over to his side.

He nodded at Vincent to begin driving when he was buckled in. Then he pressed a button and a tinted glass pane came out of the front seats to enclose the area between Vincent and us, giving us privacy. Collins raised his eyebrows, unbuckled his seat and slid to me, taking my face in his hands and kissing me hungrily. "Ah, all I thought about today was you," he said. "I wanted you to come with me to Chicago so badly, I should have insisted. Instead I get your weird phone message and it scared me so much I had to rush back." He took a deep breath and said. "You know you nearly gave me a heart attack?"

He lifted me so I was sitting in his lap with my arms around his neck. I nuzzled my face into his. "I'm glad you're back," I smiled up at him.

"Me too," he kissed the top of my nose. "Baby, why did you call me like that? What's going on?"

I dropped my head on his shoulders and sighed. "Collins, I'm not who I thought I was. I mean, I've been trying to be this perfect girl, this perfect daughter. A good girl, the girl who was generous and kind and worked so hard to put everyone's interests ahead of her own, that I didn't see what it was doing to me."

"But Baby," Collins said, entwining my fingers through his. "You are perfect for me, you're my angel, the Susan to my Daggers. You help me deal with my demons in a way no one else can."

Saving You Saving Me (You & Me Trilogy)

"But I'm not perfect, Collins," I said. "I'm perfectly flawed. That's what has me so upset. I'm not this perfect girl you thought I was. I have demons myself that I don't even know about. I've literally just found out a few hours ago that Dad was not my real father. That I was born from an inconsequential sex act between my mom and some boy, the first boy who paid her any attention."

Collins stared at me for a moment, surprise registering in his beautiful face. He didn't respond so I continued on.

"On top of that...I don't know why I broke down like that at Sawyer House. I don't know why every time we get to the point of wanting to have sex, I freeze, I break down. It isn't as though I don't want to because I do, very much with you, Collins." I took his hand and kissed his palm and rested his hand to my cheeks where I held it lovingly. Then I raised my eyes to meet his icy blue ones.

What I saw chilled my heart. Collins was looking down at his hands. He had removed his hand from my cheek and was gripping his knees and rocking.

"Collins?" I asked. "What's wrong?"

Kailin Gow

"You're not an angel?" he asked in a little lost boy's voice. "You don't want to make love to me because I scare you. You're afraid of me. I'm dirty, too dirty for you."

"No, Daggers," I said, trying to address the poor lost boy in Collins. "I don't think you're dirty. You're beautiful...so beautiful it hurts when I think how much I love you. I want you, I want you to make love to me someday, but I'm afraid. It's something within me. It's me, Daggers. Something about me that is holding back. Not you." I pulled his face to mine and kissed him gently on his lips.

He didn't respond, but kept looking at my eyes, with that empty gaze. I kissed him, holding him in my arms, stroking his hair, hugging him tightly until slowly his expression changed back to Collins. He turned his head towards me and calmly said, "Let's go home."

Chapter 21

He gently grabbed my hand and held onto it until we arrived at his mansion.

It was when we were climbing out of the car and headed up the stairs to the living room, that I turned to him and said, "How could I forget to ask, but where's Tate, your brother? Wasn't he supposed to come home with you?"

At the mention of his brother's name, Collins' face filled with anger. "Let's not mention him ever again," he said quietly.

I saw him hunch his back and all of a sudden, I realized how tired he was. I walked over to him, took off his coat, and began massaging his back. "I don't know what happened, but I'm sorry to hear it did not work out."

He walked away from me, went to the kitchen and took out two wine glasses. He walked down to the cellars and came back up the stairs, holding a chilled bottle of wine. He popped the cork and poured one glass. He was about to pour another glass for me, but said, "I was going to give you some wine, but you're not even of age to have it." He said it bitterly and I cringed inside. Was he angry at me?

"I'll have some," I said.

"I can't offer you any, Sam," he said. "You're not of drinking age."

"When did you care about that?" I asked, feeling like I'd done something wrong.

"Since when I found you in the arms of a younger man. How old is Mr. Psych? 19 or 20? Someone much closer to your age than me?"

"Collins, that's not it at all. You're not much older than me."

"But we're worlds apart in experiences, aren't we?" Collins said, taking a sip from the glass.

"Why are we having this conversation?" I asked.

Collins closed his eyes and looked pained. He bunched his fists and pounded on the counter. "Because Sam," he said in an anguished voice. "I want to keep you, but I can't. You're the woman of my dreams, but I can't hold onto you. I'm dark, I have needs that are dark, and I've tried to keep it from surfacing."

I watched in horror as Collins went on, "Susan knows how dark Daggers is. Susan knows that Daggers is holding on by the thin threads of his life to some kind of dignity, some kind of peace, if only he can stop his addiction."

"Daggers," I said approaching Collins/Daggers. "I'm here. I'm Susan. You don't need your addictions, you don't need to be abused in your relationships with women. You can have a healthy one with the girl you love who loves you just as much."

Collins/Daggers fixed me a gaze with his ice blue eyes that was so piercing, I couldn't move. "You know what happened in Chicago? I got there, and it was a seedy part of town where the jail was kept, but I had to go. Tate, my 14-year-old half-brother was being let out of jail for good behavior. He's only 14, and he has a rap sheet that could set him for life. I tried to get him out because he's the only family I think I have. I spent hundreds of thousands on lawyers to get him out. I used my influences to try to get him released on probation. We would have gotten him released today except for some legalities that came up. I would have my lawyers fight it, but then I thought of you."

"Me?"

"I thought how can I bring home a kid who was as troubled as I was when I was a kid, another Daggers to you. How can I do that to you? I'm already a handful for you, Sam." He ran his hand through his hair. "At his age, Sam, I was already sexually promiscuous. He's a hormonally-charged young virile man who spent months in jail, and you're God's gift to man – you're like Venus, to a sex-starved man. I began worrying about your safety with him around."

"He's only 14," I said.

"Doesn't matter," Collins said. "His body doesn't know that when he reacts to seeing you."

"Collins..." I said, making a face. "You overestimate my appeal."

"No, I don't," he said. "You don't even realize how men react around you, Sam. Michael's a pastor, and he's practically throwing himself at you. Mr. Psych can't keep his hands off you..."

"So you're going to let him stay in jail?" I asked.

"Until I can figure out how to get him help, without putting you at risk."

"The longer he's in jail, the worst his influences. He's going to learn worst criminal behavior..."

"I know, and at the same time, I think he should stay there. Luckily most of what he's done is due to the need to eat and survive – theft and other crimes. Not that I'm excusing it, but at least he hasn't physically harmed anyone."

"So you were hoping to enroll him at Cliffside Academy?" I asked looking bewildered.

"Seems like a nice school with teachers who are good with keeping students in line," Collins said smiling. "Alright, Cliffside Academy would be the ideal school to enroll him, and Principal Lowry seems to like me," Collins said. "I would see no problem getting Tate enrolled in school, and with a pretty tutor to help him get up to speed..."

"Me," I said. "The bait to get him to stay in school and to get him studying..."

"Hire the straight-A pretty girl who needed a scholarship to college to tutor and attract the ex-con brother of mine. Call it an internship or whatever, but then Tate would have an instant friend and maybe a girlfriend."

"That's why you asked if I had friends or a boyfriend that day," I said. I closed my eyes and tears of anger spilled from the corners. "You were going to use me, prostitute me to your brother." I wanted to scream, to beat his chest with my fists. I wanted to go to the corner of the room and sob until I couldn't cry any longer. How could Collins be so cruel? How could he think people can be bought like that? But then that's what he'd known all his life. He had warned me that's all he'd known.

Collins was standing there, his back pressed against the table, staring at me with his pale icy blue eyes. They were glistening with unshed tears. "You're looking at me like I'm a two-headed monster," he said. "I probably deserve that, but you have to know something about me. I had planned all this out, but when you bumped into me and fell into my arms looking so cute, sweet, and flustered; I fell in love with you then. All thoughts of any boy or man touching you, sent rage throughout my body. I couldn't bear thinking of it. I didn't even think about whether or not

Saving You Saving Me (You & Me Trilogy)

you fit into the typical type of lovers I had. I didn't care
about that for the first time in my life."

"Until now?" I asked, my voice husky and sad.

Collins looked down, ashamed. "Every time we
touch, every time we kiss; it becomes torture for me. I want
to go all the way with you, but I can't because I'm afraid to
scare you. I'm afraid you'll react like you did before, break
down. I don't know if it's truly because of a subconscious
fear you may have of having sex with a freak or if it's
something that happened to you." He walked over to me
and pulled me into his arms then. "I want to be there for
you, I really do, but baby, I can't handle being this close to
you and not being able to touch you like I want to…You
know I have a fragile ego, and I'm still fighting for control
over my desires…"

"Oh Collins," I cried. "I'll still be here for you."

"No, that's not enough Sam. With your issues and
my issues; this may not work out. It's too much. I'm so so
sorry, Sam."

My heart sank, and I couldn't get up. Collins
couldn't even look at me as he left the room. I must have
been crying all night when Mrs. Anderson came and got me

from the ground. She fed me breakfast and helped me get dressed, and then she called for Vincent to drive me back to my parents' house. My suitcases had already been packed and loaded. I was no longer part of his life.

Moments That Change Your Life – This was the First

I was 13-years-old when my father caught me and Billy in the music room, with Billy's 14-year-old inexperienced hands all over my half-dressed body. Worse, his pants were down, and his thing was out. He was rubbing it against my panties and pushing his hips up and down against mine. It felt strange and uncomfortable, and I did not want to be there, but if I didn't, he would go on with his endless teasing and bullying. Months of harassing me and threatening me with harm if I told anyone about what he had planned, until I gave in and was going to let him have his way with me. He had me pinned down on the table while he tried to undress me. He had torn off my t-shirt and had pushed up my training bra so that my breasts were bared while his hands groped at them roughly.

Saving You Saving Me (You & Me Trilogy)

"I don't want this," I cried. "Stop it now, Billy!"

"You can't tease me like that and expect me not to finish what I came for," he sneered and then slapped me hard across the face. I struggled to get out from under him, but he slapped me again, saying, "Just because your daddy is a pastor doesn't mean you don't like this too. You're a whore like any girl. You're no better than anyone else, bitch." He took his hands and shoved my panties down my legs, and was hovering above me when a familiar voice yelled at him, and yanked him off me. Father stood there panting as he looked from Billy to me and to Billy again. Father's normally ruddy face turned a shade redder, clearly showing how angry he was. He didn't say anything, but yanked Billy by the collar, pushed him, and told him to stay away from me and to never touch me again. If he caught him near me again or on the property, he'd call the cops on him. He wasn't going to tolerate any boy molesting his daughter right on his church property.

Billy was scared of course, being only 14, so he ran and I never saw him or his family at church again.

Dad then grabbed me by the collar, tried to push down my t-shirt, took me to the family restroom, took some soap and proceeded to wash my mouth out with it.

That wasn't the worst part. What was worse was the way Dad looked at me – disgusted and with shame. His perfect pretty little princess was a slut, a whore, at 13, having sex with a trashy boy like Billy at her father's own church. How would he be able to live down the shame?

I had never seen him so angry. Mother had to intervene, pull him away before he did anything drastic. I was trembling like a leaf, feeling my whole body shake until I was exhausted. I didn't want to think about what Billy did. I didn't want to think about how he made me feel. I just wanted to be held, to have my parents assure me I was alright, that I was safe, and that whatever Billy did would never ever happen to me again.

That didn't happen. Dad never looked me in the eye from then on, and instead of seeing Billy as the monster, I began thinking the monster was I.

*****

Epilogue

<u>**Today**</u>

I remember Daggers' words to me the day he left: "Chances are everything. Seize them when you can, because those are the moments that make life worth living."

Life is measured in moments. Moments are measured by chance, and chances are everything. Had I not been at Dr. Green's office the day after I turned eighteen, this story would have been very different. Dangerously different. I thought I was the one who was doing all the saving, but in reality, the opposite was true.

Daggers/Collins came by to visit me at my parents' house a month after he broke up with me and took me to the beach so we could talk. He was dress in faded jeans and a plaid shirt, while I wore a pink ruffled summer dress. It was awkward, and we both looked like hell, having lost weight. Dressed like that, he looked very young, close to 19 or 20. "I've missed you," he said reaching for my hand.

"I've missed you, too," I said, gulping down the tears that threatened to spill down my face.

"Sammy baby," he said reaching for my hand as we walked along the beach, "I wanted to tell you that I'll have to go to Europe for a while for business. I'm setting up a subsidiary there, a business office, so I'll be gone for a good month or two."

I felt numb. Why was he telling me this? Was he trying to torture me?

He leaned in to give me a quick kiss on my cheek and said, "I want you to have this. It's the key to my heart." He pressed it into my hands. "You have my heart already, you might as well have everything else."

That's when I had a waterworks of tears spill all over my face. He kissed away my tears and pulled me in close to his chest and held me tight. "We've come a long ways, baby. You and I. But we still have some distance to cover, hurdles to jump, if you want to." He laughed his soft gentle Daggers laugh that always sent flutters to my stomach. "I'm a many-layered SOB, a real messed up nut job, who others have given up on, yet you...you continue to peel away the layers." He played with my hair and kissed my forehead. I sighed. My multi-layered Daggers. Each layer more intriguing than the last, each one bringing me closer to the edge of no return.

"I want to peel away those layers," I protested. "I want to know who you are, deep down, if you'll let me."

Daggers closed his eyes for a moment and inhaled sharply. "I know, Sam, and I've been fighting it. If you knew what's really hidden behind all those layers, you'd stay away from me as far away from me as possible." He opened his eyes to look at me earnestly. "You deserve to know, though. And I'm giving you that chance. With the key...the key to my safe deposit box. But once you know, there's no going back."

*****

Was it fate that brought two people together who so desperately needed each other or was it random chance?

I've known Daggers for only two months, but I felt as though I've known him for a lifetime. We've been through so much together and have come a good ways. But as he said, there is still a ways to go. As much as he believed that I saved him from his dark demons, he had ended up saving me. Now there was no way I was turning my back on him now.

I took the key he placed in my hands and went to his bank to retrieve the safe deposit box within.

It was one he had set up under my name. My Collins, my Daggers was so considerate, so giving. When I slid the key into the lock, I held my breath. I didn't know what to expect.

I lifted the lid of the box and found a note from Collins.

"Sam, I love you so much, but I know my past will come up to haunt you as it has already reared its ugly head. I can't shield you from all of it, but I'll try my best. I'm afraid discovering Daggers' secret was one layer you got through, but there is one I have to reveal so you know why I'm far more messed up than I seem. My mother was so abusive I finally ran away from home when I was 13, and I was living on the streets, having to do things that I wasn't proud of, just to survive. I want to be with you, and I want to come clean to you about everything, if you'll give me

Saving You Saving Me (You & Me Trilogy)

that chance, I'm laying it out for you here. After listening to these tapes, if you still want me, I'm yours. If not, then go ahead, take the money that is in the enclosed envelope. One million dollars should be enough to cover many things I think you deserve to have, especially a college education, should you decide to take the other route, which I pray to God you won't take. The choice is yours."

You & Me Series continues with Sam, Daggers, Derek, and Collins in Book 2

Finding You Finding Me

Available at All Bookstores

Kailin Gow

Saving You Saving Me Playlist

http://pl.st/p/23138740235

Participate in the
Saving You Saving Me Project

http://www.SavingYouSavingMe.com

Saving You Saving Me (You & Me Trilogy)
Resources

Saving YOU Saving ME brings up several social subjects since it takes place at a crisis teen and young adult call center. While the advice given through the scenarios Samantha Sullivan encounters at the fictional Sawyer House is a good starting point to explore the actual issues, here is a list of resources to help you or a friend learn more about some of the issues brought up in this book:

Cutting/Self-Injury

http://www.mayoclinic.com/health/self-injury/DS00775

http://kidshealth.org/teen/your_mind/mental_health/cutting.html

Bullying

http://www.stopbullying.gov/

http://kidshealth.org/teen/your_mind/problems/bullies.html#cat20139

Peer Pressure

Kailin Gow

http://teenadvice.about.com/cs/peerpressure/a/blpeerpressure.htm

http://teens.webmd.com/peer-pressure

Teen Pregnancy

http://www.thenationalcampaign.org/

Drug Use

http://www.drugabuse.gov/publications/infofacts/understanding-drug-abuse-addiction

http://www.drugabuse.gov/

Alcoholism

http://kidshealth.org/teen/drug_alcohol/alcohol/coping_alcoholic.html#cat20139

http://www.mayoclinic.com/health/alcoholism/DS00340

Saving You Saving Me (You & Me Trilogy)

<u>Self-Esteem/Self-Image</u>
<u>http://kidshealth.org/kid/feeling/emotion/self_esteem.html#</u>
<u>cat20139</u>
<u>http://www.mayoclinic.com/health/self-esteem/MH00128</u>

<u>Abuse</u>
<u>http://www.helpguide.org/mental/domestic_violence_abuse</u>
<u>_help_treatment_prevention.htm</u>

<u>http://www.childhelp.org/</u>

Kailin Gow

Want to Know More about *Saving You Saving Me (You & Me Trilogy)*, Author Insight, Author Appearance, Contests and Giveaways?

Get a Free Full-length Book when you subscribe to Kailin's newsletter!

https://dl.bookfunnel.com/5rmis5rrj1

Saving YOU Saving ME

Book Club Discussion Questions

1. Samantha has her heart set on becoming either a Counselor or Psychiatrist. Do you think that is why she is drawn to Daggers or is it because she subconsciously relates to him?

2. In Samantha's narration of the story, she brings up Sigmund Freud's id and ego, personified by Lola and Serious Susan. **Lola** represents Sam's id, the instinctive and primitive side of her unconsciousness that is driven by the "**Pleasure Principle**" which strives for immediate gratification of all desires, wants, and needs such as hunger, thirst, anger, and sex. If these needs are not satisfied immediately, the result is a state of anxiety or tension.

   Serious Susan represents Sam's ego, which operates on the **"Reality Principle"** – the part of our human consciousness that strives to satisfy the id with realistic and socially appropriate ways such

Kailin Gow

as delayed gratification – acting on the behavior
during an appropriate time and place.

At one point, Samantha even uses the name "Susan"
as her alias at Sawyer House. Do you think it was a
conscious move or unconscious? As she talks to
Daggers as Susan, did she act on her Lola side or
Susan side?

3. How did her feelings for Daggers finally raise
   itself? In a dream? In her conversations with him?

4. Why do you think Samantha had a nervous
   breakdown?

5. Who is more messed up? Daggers, Samantha,
   Collins, Derek, or Samantha's mother Mrs.
   Sullivan? Why?

6. Daggers mentioned Sam had peeled one layer of
   him, but he is darker than that. What do you think
   he is trying to hide from Samantha, but feels he
   must reveal in order to have their relationship work
   for them?

Saving You Saving Me (You & Me Trilogy)
7. Should Samantha confront her father about the Billy Incident?

Kailin Gow

A Sneak Peak at an Upcoming New Contemporary
Romance Series from Kailin Gow:

Loving

Summer

kailin gow

Saving You Saving Me (You & Me Trilogy)

Description

Summer has always looked forward to spending her summers at her Aunt's beach house with the Donovans. To her, summers at Aunt Sookie's beach house was magical, especially getting to spend time with the Donovans - her best friend Rachel and Rachel's brothers Nathaniel, and Drew. Here at Aunt Sookie's beach house, they can be anyone and anything they dreamed. For Summer, she had always wished to become as pretty as Rachel and for her brothers to think of her as more than Rachel's friend. For Nat and Drew, summers at Aunt Sookie's beach house meant fun and escape, a place where they go to with their mom and sister for the summer, away from city life. They never thought this summer would be different. They never thought things would change as much as they did...and it all began with them falling for and loving Summer. A YA contemporary romance with an edge.

Available at all Bookstores!

Chapter 1

<u>Summer</u>

I'm standing by the baggage claim area, waiting for my three friends to arrive, and wondering a little if maybe I should have made one of those large cards with their names on that people occasionally hold up. It at least keeps me from wondering what it's going to be like when they arrive. Oh God, I don't think I've been this nervous since... well, forever.

The card is out. I don't have one to write on, and anyway, I sent Rachel my picture. I wonder if she was surprised about how much I've changed. I mean, the last time I saw her, I still had my braces in, and boys didn't give me a second glance. She was always the pretty one, even if she did like to hide it.

It's been so *long* since I saw her. Any of them. It used to be that I'd spend practically every day with Rachel, because Aunt Sookie babysat her and the others, or

Saving You Saving Me (You & Me Trilogy)

Rachel's mother would look after me while Aunt Sookie was busy with her acting academy. I guess none of us need that now, but we can still surf the way we used to, or go to the beach, or anything. When we all used to stay over at Aunt Sookie's place on the beach every summer, it used to be great.

It's been three years now though. Maybe it won't be so good. Maybe I won't even know Rachel so much. We've talked on the phone and online, but a friend you spend all summer with is different to one you just talk to now and again, right? I haven't seen any of the Donovans since they moved away to San Francisco. And what about Drew? What about *Nat*? I wonder what he thought about the picture I sent. Did he like it? Did he see that I'm not some little girl anymore?

"Summer?"

There's a Goth girl coming towards me, all purple streaked black hair, ivory skin and dark makeup, in a t-shirt and jeans that go with her hair like someone has streaked purple dye on them. I stare at her for a good couple of seconds before I see her face fully and rush forward to hug her.

"Rachel!"

I shouldn't have worried about what it's going to be like with her back. Just hugging her, I *know*. I know that we're exactly the friends we always were. Okay, so she's done something freaky with her hair, but she's still Rachel. We have *so* much to catch up on. I step back from her just so that I can look at her, and I can see her doing the same. It's like we're re-learning what we look like, or something.

"Wow," Rachel says. "You've grown taller, and you're in great shape."

"Volleyball," I explain. "*Competitive* volleyball. Mom thought it would be great for me to pick up a team sport, so I went for that one."

"You always were better at doing what your mom wanted than me," Rachel says. She smiles while she says it, but she's told me about a lot of it.

"You still aren't seeing eye to eye with her?" I ask. Maybe I should join the diplomatic core after this.

"No, Mom's being a bitch." Rachel's expression darkens, which given the way she looks now is a pretty scary sight. "Ever since she caught Dad screwing around, it's been the same." She shakes her head, and the expression passes, just like that. Maybe it's because it's such a great day no one can stay angry for long. "I don't care, though. I'm here with you, the beach, and Aunt Sookie!"

I hug her tightly again. I've missed Rachel so much. She's like the sister I never had. Talking of siblings…

"Where are Drew and Nat?" I ask with a grin. "You didn't abandon them at the San Francisco airport, did you?"

"I wish. They're here somewhere. There. There they are." Rachel waves over at them and I can't help staring. Drew's grown. He must be over six foot now, and he has the muscles to go with it, not really concealed by the plain white t-shirt he wears with his blue jeans. I remember him as scrawny, maybe cute in a kind of way, but nothing like this. As for Nat, he's even taller, though maybe not as broadly built as his brother these days. He's wearing a white t-shirt under a blue and white plaid shirt with loose fitting jeans and boots. They suit him. That deep copper hair of his seems to shine in the sunlight. I can't help staring as the two of them get closer.

"Could you maybe not stare at my brothers in open mouthed admiration?" Rachel whispers. "It will only make their egos bigger."

That's hard to do, especially with Nat. Drew... well, he's impressive, and who would have thought that he'd have turned into some kind of gorgeous hunk in just three years, but Nat was my first real boyfriend. My first kiss. I can remember when he used to defend me from the bullies back in kindergarten. He shouldn't be allowed to go around looking like some kind of rock star.

"Summer?" Drew says as they get close. "I'd hardly recognize you if you hadn't sent Rachel that photo."

I can't help looking at him, at how much he's changed. "Three years makes a big difference."

"Nah," Nat says, and his voice is a little deeper than it was. It sounds more self-assured. "You're all still babies compared with me. Good to see you again, Summer."

I glance at Rachel. She knows. She knows exactly how big a crush I've always had on Nat. Okay, so it didn't go anywhere after I kissed him, but I wanted it to. I wanted it to so bad. Just from the way Drew's looking at me, he knows too. About the only one who doesn't seem to is Nat.

Nat throws an arm around my shoulders and I feel myself start to blush. That's just him. Being near him.

Saving You Saving Me (You & Me Trilogy)

"You're taller than you used to be," he says. "I won't have to bend down to talk to you."

Or kiss me, I think, but I stop myself from saying it. I manage to make a joke of it. "Oh, come on, I was never that much shorter than you."

"Midget," Nat said simply, his smile widening.

"I was *not* a midget."

Nat raises an eyebrow. "It looked that way from up here. The same as Rachel. The Two Midgets of Malibu."

"It's not our fault if you're just unnaturally tall," Rachel shoots back, and that starts off a brief argument about exactly what kind of height counts as unnatural. I've missed this. I've missed *them*.

"Do you remember the time Aunt Sookie decided to teach Nat to surf?" I say, while they collect their bags.

"Of course I remember it," Rachel says with a wicked smile. From the way Nat looks suddenly uncomfortable, I guess he remembers it too. "He looked like someone had tried to drown him by the time he came in."

"Those waves were big," Nat protests.

"Sure they were," Drew says. "Though mostly not right on the beach."

Kailin Gow

Pretty soon, they're all talking about the old times we had at the beach house. There were the plays we'd put on right on the beach when we'd spent too much time around Aunt Sookie's Acting Academy, and the beach fires where we'd roast marshmallows, and a dozen other things. Some of them, like playing at being pirates in the surf, were just kids' things. Some of them, like that kiss with Nat, definitely weren't.

"Do you remember the time we decided that a beach house wasn't enough," Rachel asks, "and we ended up camping out on the beach maybe twenty feet from the door?"

I nod. I can remember all of it, from the stars above us then to trying to erect a tent that kept falling down around us through the night. We always had the best time at the beach house when we were kids. It's hard to believe that we've left it so long before doing this again. Will this time live up to it? I smile as I realize it will, because the most important thing is that we're all here. That's what matters.

I lead the way out into the airport parking lot. It's a huge place, and it takes a while to find my car. When we do, the others seem impressed by the huge, shining black expanse of the Grand Cherokee.

"This is yours?" Nat asks like he can't quite believe it.

I shrug. "Mom and Dad want me to be safe out on the road. I guess they thought that an SUV would do it, and Aunt Sookie pitched in to get this one."

"Well, short of a truck, I guess there isn't much bigger than you out there," Rachel says.

"That's the idea." They pile in, and Rachel gets the passenger seat. I'm kind of glad of that. Having Nat beside me would be too much of a distraction as I drive us out of LAX, through the constant traffic that's there on the way out towards Malibu. The beach house is out on the Pacific Coast Highway, and we can see the pier from it, with all the surfers gathered nearby, waiting for the waves to be perfect for them. Maybe we'll join them in a while.

Rachel certainly seems excited about that possibility. "I can't wait to get to the beach and into a swimsuit," she says. "Do you know what the temperature was when we left? Sixty degrees. That is not the right temperature for summer. I want to be out on the beach getting tanned."

"There are tanned Goths?" Drew asks. I'd forgotten what it can be like with the two of them, constantly bickering in that way that says they really love one another as deeply as only twins can. It must be nice having brothers and sisters who are that close. In fact, I know how good it can be, because I've had that with them before. I've been that extra sister, as close to any of them as they are to each other. Maybe I'll have that again this summer.

Maybe I'll have other things too. I have to admit, the thought of Nat in board shorts is pretty good.

"We can do that," I say. "We'll get back to the beach house and head straight for the ocean, if you like."

"That does sound pretty good," Drew says. "I don't know how long it's been since I last surfed. I used to love being able to just go out and surf first thing in the morning before breakfast."

"That or running along the beach, while the sun's still coming up," Nat says, and I can picture him doing it. It's only half a memory, because it's not him three years ago that I'm picturing. It's him now, looking gorgeous as he does it.

Saving You Saving Me (You & Me Trilogy)

"So you aren't both ready to rush home to everything back there?" Rachel asks, and I can tell that it's some kind of private joke between the three of them.

"Are you kidding?" Drew asks. "I'd forgotten how good Malibu could be."

I can see Nat in the rearview mirror, and he's smiling. "I think it could be pretty good here," he admits. "Okay, so there are things I'm going to miss about San Francisco, but they'll still be there when I get back."

"And for now, there's the beach," Drew adds.

I can't help laughing at that. I guess when you live somewhere every day you forget just how wonderful it can be. Or maybe you forget just how good some of the other things in the world are, like great friends.

"You know," I say. "I've really missed all of you. I've missed *this*."

Rachel nods. "I've missed it too."

www.ingramcontent.com/pod-product-compliance
Lightning Source LLC
Chambersburg PA
CBHW052032240626
47153CB00006B/2052